D0277086

YOU DESERVE NOTHING

YOU DESERVE NOTHING

Alexander Maksik

JOHN MURRAY

First published in Great Britain in 2011 by John Murray (Publishers)
An Hachette UK Company

1

An excerpt from this novel
was first published in Narrative magazine.

A CIP catalogue record for this title is available from the British Library

Hardback ISBN 978-1-84854-570-0
Trade Paperback ISBN 978-1-84854-571-7
Ebook ISBN 978-1-84854-573-1

Printed and bound by Clays Ltd, St Ives plc

John Murray policy is to use papers that are natural, renewable and recyclable products and made from wood grown in sustainable forests. The logging and manufacturing processes are expected to conform to the environmental regulations of the country of origin.

John Murray (Publishers)
338 Euston Road
London NW1 3BH

www.johnmurray.co.uk

For my parents

And in memory of Tom Johnson

I do not want to choose between
the right and wrong sides of the world,
and I do not like a choice to be made.

—ALBERT CAMUS

GILAD
24 YEARS OLD

You live in one place. The next day you live somewhere else. It isn't complicated. You get on a plane. You get off. People are always talking about home. Their houses. Their neighborhoods. In movies, it's where they came from, where they came up. The movies are full of that stuff. The street. The block. The diner. Italian movies. Black movies. Jewish movies. Brooklyn or whatever.

But I never really got that. The streets were never running through my blood. I never loved a house. So, all that nothing-like-home stuff doesn't really register. The way you can be living in one place and then in a few hours you can be living somewhere else, that's what I think about when I think about home. You wake up, do what you do, eat, go to sleep, wake up, eat, Monday, Tuesday, Wednesday, Thursday, Friday, Saturday. The same thing for days, months, years and then, one day, you're no longer there.

People always say how hard it must be to move from place to place. It isn't.

When I got here I was seventeen. We moved from Riyadh where we'd been living for nearly two years. I had three weeks to pack my things, to "prepare" myself. That was my father—three weeks to "prepare" myself. I don't know what that means really. It took me an hour to pack my bags. I didn't tell anyone at school I was moving.

The year ended, I kicked around the pool for a while and then we were on a plane and gone. That's just the way it happened. I didn't feel much of anything. I was only amazed again that a world simply disappears behind you, that one life becomes another life becomes another life becomes another.

And then we lived in Paris.

We lived in Dubai, Shanghai, Tokyo, Kuala Lumpur, Seoul, Jerusalem and Riyadh.

And then we lived in Paris. And Paris was different because it was the last place we moved as a family. The last place imposed upon me.

WILL
38 YEARS OLD

The optimism, the sense of possibility and hope comes at the end of August. There are new pens, unmarked novels, fresh textbooks, and promises of a better year. The season of reflection is not January but June. Another year passed, the students gone, the halls silent. You're left there alone. The quiet of a school emptied for the summer is that of a hotel closed for winter, a library closed for the night, ghosts swirling through the rooms.

There is the quick disintegration. The bell rings and the whole thing explodes into the bright day. You walk into the sunshine, dazed by the light.

* * *

The windows are open. I'm in the corner of the room. The June breeze sways the poplars on the far edge of the field. The halls are quiet, the students in assembly.

On the walls are fifteen portraits of the Bundren family. There's a poster advertising a forgotten RSC production of *Macbeth,* the Cartier-Bresson photograph of Jean-Paul Sartre with Jean Pouillon on the Pont des Arts. There's another of Sartre at the Café de Flore, the photograph of Camus smoking a cigarette, an old *Cool Hand Luke* poster and one for the premiere of *After Hours.* There's Tommie Smith and John Carlos on the

Olympic podium—heads bowed, fists raised. Laurence Olivier as Hamlet and a bulletin board covered with poems, Hemingway standing with Sylvia Beach in front of Shakespeare & Company.

A steel desk sits at the front of the room. It is, like everything else here, worn and broken. Heavy gray curtains hang from an ancient and long defunct pulley line. Fluorescent lights, thin brown carpet. All of it in the style of seventies-era American public schools—generic and shabby.

There are two identical floors—long corridors lined with metal lockers and classrooms. A high black steel security gate surrounds the school. Once you're inside you might as well be in Phoenix.

With the breeze moving through, my classroom is cool. In a few hours the buildings will be drained of students and with them will go all their noise and theater. Everything is finished, essays graded, final reports written.

The last day of school. We return final exams. We say goodbye. They clear out their things, buses arrive and the broken building falls into silence.

* * *

I'm waiting for my first period sophomores. There are classes like these—students possessed of grace and kindness and intelligence, all thrown together for the year. They arrive and you know. You become a family. It is a kind of love affair.

At the far end of the school they're streaming out of the auditorium from assembly. Mr. Spencer has already wished them a good summer. He's read them something—a quotation, a poem he's found inspirational. Mr. Goring scratches the back of his head as he reviews the day's schedule. He reminds them that all lockers must be empty. There will be trashcans in the halls. Please use them. Respect your school, students. Do not run. Please, no running.

Released, they come up the hallway, some wave as they pass my room.

"What up, Mr. S?"

"Have a good summer, Mr. S, try not to party too hard."

Julia comes in pulling her blond curly hair back into a ponytail.

She's the first.

"Last day of school," I say.

"Oh really? Is it?" She rolls her eyes.

"That's what I've heard. Pretty sad."

She nods.

I sit on my desk and sort through a stack of exams until I find hers.

"So," I say.

"So, listen Mr. S. I'm going to miss you this summer and I want you to know that I really loved your class and that I think you're a great teacher." She blushes. "So, thank you for every-thing. You kind of changed my life this year."

"Thank you, Julia. I've loved having you as my student."

She looks at the floor.

Steven Connor struts into the classroom, short and bluff and pushing his chest out.

"Mr. S!" He says, extending his hand, a little businessman. "How you doing, Mr. S. You know I'm going to miss this class, dude. Why don't you teach juniors? You suck. What the hell am I going to do next year?"

He cocks his head to the side and looks me in the eye. We shake hands. Then he notices Julia.

"Wait, am I like, interrupting something?"

Julia giggles. "No, Steve."

Mazin, a thin, grinning Jordanian, runs into the room and throws his arms around me.

9

"Dude, Mr. S. *Dude.* Are we going to hang this summer? Because I'm *so* going to miss this class, man. But it's cool, you're coming to my party right? You got the invitation?"

"I'm coming. I'll be there. Sunday night. I'm there."

The classroom slowly fills.

I sit on the edge of my desk as I always do. I look around the room and face them. They expect something from me, some conclusion, some official end to the year.

I push myself from the desk and stand.

"Last day of school. A few minutes left in our year together. I have your exams and I'll give them to you before you leave but I want to tell you a few things first. I want you to know that it isn't often that I have a class like yours. I was very lucky this year. You're exceptional. You've been honest, kind, funny, adventurous, open and generous. You've been passionate and interested and you have come here day after day after day always willing to consider the things I've said to you. My dream as a teacher has always been to walk into my classroom, sit down and participate in an intelligent, exciting discussion of literature and philosophy. We are smart people sitting in a room talking about beautiful things, ugly and difficult things. You've been that class. I'm grateful to you. You've reminded me of why I'm here and I've loved teaching you."

Julia begins to cry. Mazin looks at his desk.

"You know what I believe is important. You know what I'll say to you about choice, about your lives, about time. You remember, I hope, the discussions we've had about "Ode on a Grecian Urn." "Ode on a Grecian Urn," which was written by whom, Mazin?"

There's a long pause. "John Keats, Mr. Silver," he says proudly.

"John Keats." I smile at him. "You'll forget most of what we've discussed in this classroom. You'll forget Wilfred Owen and *The Grapes of Wrath* and Thoreau and Emerson and Blake and the difference between romance and Romanticism, Romanticism and Transcendentalism. It will all become a blur, a swirl of information, which adds to that spreading swamp in your brain. That's fine. What you must not forget, however, are the questions these writers compelled you to ask yourselves— questions of courage, of passion and belief. And do not forget this."

I stop. It is very quiet. A locker slams in the hallway. Classes are shortened today and I know the bell will ring soon. I look at them. I mean it all, but teaching is also performance.

"What?" Steven asks. "Dude, we don't have time. What? Don't forget what?"

"*This*. Don't forget what it felt like. All of us here. What happened in this room. How much you've changed since you walked through the door, morons that you were, nine months ago."

They laugh.

"Thank you. Thank you for all of it." There is the moment of quiet and then, as if orchestrated, the bell rings.

They stay in their seats. There are other students in the hallways. Lockers slamming closed. I pick up their exams and call their names. They hug me. Mazin first. He pushes the side of his head against my chest. They thank me. They wish me a good summer. I can't speak. They file out into the hall and disappear into the summer.

It was, I think, my best year.

* * *

That afternoon there's a barbeque for the faculty. Tables on the grass. A PA playing bad disco meant to be ironic. The kind of thing teachers shouldn't be listening to at school. Shouldn't be listening to anywhere. Champagne in plastic cups.

From my office window I can see them collecting around the

hors d'oeuvres table. Jean-Paul, who runs the cafeteria, walks around grinning with a tray of *kirs*. I'm putting off the walk down the stairs and across the grass to the party. I don't want to pretend to care what they're doing for the summer. I don't want to drink cheap champagne and smile. I don't want to play softball. So I stay in my office and clean out my desk. I file papers—notes from students, parents. Articles I want to save, poems, short stories. I throw away old quizzes, letters from the College Board.

The halls are silent. The last buses have rolled out of the parking lot taking the students away. There are papers and pens lying on the floor, trash cans overflowing, a pile of for-gotten clothes, an old lunch rotting in a paper bag, *The Catcher in the Rye* with its cover torn off.

When my desk is clean—pens in their cup, books lined up, drawers emptied—I walk out into the hall and down the stairs toward the picnic. Nothing left to do. No classes to prepare, nothing to grade, no one who needs to talk.

* * *

Later I sit on the grass with Mia, drinking champagne. She hands me her cup and raises her arms. Released from its pins, her hair spills down her back. Light brown, but now in the sun nearly red. Mia, so calm here, so sure of herself, and so off balance in the city.

Her face in repose falls to a frown and sitting alone in a café she is rarely approached. Only the most brazen strangers talk to her and they're the least appealing. They frighten and offend her, these men who believe a pretty woman has the obligation to smile, that she owes the world her beauty.

Even the way she pins it, there are always pieces coming

undone, strands of hair falling around her neck, grazing her cheek.

We sit with our shoes off. She's leaning back on her elbows.

"So, that was the year."

"Thank God," she says without opening her eyes. "I'm so tired. You?"

"Exhausted. But it was good and I'm sad. I'll miss those kids. A lot of them."

"They love you. You're changing lives," she laughs. "You're a life changer."

I shake my head

"You know it's true. They love you. You're a cult leader."

Just then Mickey Gold lumbers over. Approaching seventy, red-faced, a wild cartoon—huge in body and gesture. The kind of man you'd expect behind a desk at a talent agency in Queens. But he's been teaching Biology here for the last thirty years and as a result he's gone slightly mad.

From ten yards out he calls, "Mia and Will! Want a refill?"

He says it again, working the rhyme, making it into a song. He comes carrying a bottle of champagne, snatched from the bar. Mia and I exchange quick glances. I like Mickey. He's exotic here, so decidedly not French, lacking in subtlety and apparently unaware of himself. He is sloppy, unmannered, and loud. Yet he speaks French fluently, punctuates his English sentences with emphatic "*ouis.*" I'm impressed and embarrassed by him.

He eases himself down onto the grass across from us. It's difficult work. He's a tall man. Six foot two, a firm and significant belly. He pats Mia's knee and says, "Another one down the shitter."

* * *

She hasn't spoken a word to Mickey since the Academic Achievement awards two weeks ago when he stood up, walked to the podium and said, "This year I'll be giving the award to a young lady who, along with being an excellent writer and a gifted, budding biologist, also happens to smell like a rose."

Mia, sitting next to me in the auditorium, let out a pained gasp and then covered her mouth with her hand.

He continued, "She's a young woman whom I was happy to see every day and whose absence in class always made me a little sad. It isn't every year that I teach a young woman whose talents are equaled by a lovely midriff. Beauty and brains. Personally, I can't wait to see what she becomes. This year's award goes to Colette Shriver."

Colette, face flushed, walked to the podium. It was to her great dismay (and to Mia's) that she was that day wearing a white T-shirt cut short enough to reveal her stomach, a small silver ring in her navel. Mickey stood at the podium smiling, arms outstretched, awaiting her with a hug and a kiss on the cheek, his nose cocked and ready for her rosy scent.

Poor Colette, mortified, momentarily swallowed up by Mickey's mighty arms. Compelled to walk to the stage, ignoring the suggestive whispers of the boys on the aisle—yeah Colette, give him some tongue.

"To reduce academic achievement to her midriff? He's a teacher! He's disgusting."

We were eating lunch together, whispering in a far corner of the cafeteria. I smiled.

"What? You think it was funny?"

"He doesn't know. He's oblivious."

"That is not an excuse. Come on, Will. He's a teacher. You know what he said was horrible. It isn't funny. He's a teacher. You shouldn't take it so lightly."

"How should I take it? He'll never change, he's been teaching for thirty years. He's harmless, no one takes him seriously, the kids mostly love him. They think he's hysterical. They also think he's a good teacher. He isn't a threat to anyone."

Mia rolled her eyes. "Of course he's a threat. Of course he's harmful. You can't just excuse him because he's old or because he's been doing the same thing for thirty years. He makes whatever good work Colette may have done unimportant. You don't celebrate a teenager's body in front of the entire school at a fucking academic achievement ceremony, O.K.?"

"You're right, of course. Still."

"No."

She'd been raising her voice steadily and a group of girls a few tables away had begun to look over at us and whisper.

We often sat together in the cafeteria and argued. We leaned in and spoke intimately about one thing or another. We were young and both famously single. Conversations like these only furthered the rumors of a secret affair. It wasn't uncommon for a brave tenth grader to raise her hand and ask, giggling, when Ms. Keller and I were getting married.

Lowering my voice, I said, "Look, I realize that what he said was inappropriate. I recognize all of that but can you not see the humor?"

"It's that attitude which has allowed him the freedom to make those comments. No one says anything. He's tolerated as a silly man. That's just Mickey. He's harmless. So he goes on commenting on his students' bodies and sniffing their perfume. I don't find him charming at all. That he's an old man oblivious to the world around him makes it no better."

"Can't I be offended and amused at the same time?"

Mia let out a frustrated breath. This kind of thing was always a source of tension for us. She was too easily offended and carried every offense with her for days.

* * *

And so now with Mickey's sudden approach and landing, Mia becomes stone.

"Right down the shitter. The years just go rolling on by," he says refilling my cup. He tilts the bottle toward Mia who has covered hers with her palm. "Mia?"

She shakes her head and says nothing. If Mickey registers this slight he gives no indication.

"So what are the big plans this summer? Going anywhere good?"

Unwilling to endure Mia's silence I answer. "Going to Greece, back mid-August. What are you up to, Mickey?"

"Greece, huh? Great great. I was in Greece oh, I don't know, twenty years ago maybe. Met a Swedish girl there. My God. What a body. The islands right? You're going to the islands?"

"Santorini."

"*Oui*. Been to Santorini. *Trés beau*. But the girls are in Mykonos my friend. Everyone's naked. Naked women and gay men. Not bad odds. I'd say go to Mykonos. See what happens. Find a girl. Not bad. Not a bad way to spend a summer. Mia? Plans?"

But Mia is already getting up. She slips her feet into her sandals and walks away. Mickey looks at me for an explanation.

"You should ask her."

"O.K. Well, women. I'll go grab her. Have a great summer, Will. Mykonos. I'm telling you. Girls for miles. You take good care of yourself, O.K.?"

"I will and thanks for the tip, Mickey. You have a great summer too."

He levers himself to his feet, groans and heads off to find Mia. She eludes him and eventually works her way back to me. I smile at her.

"You're a bad person," she says, forgiving me.

* * *

Mia and I together on the *métro* home with old shopping bags on the seats opposite us. They're full of end-of-the-year gifts—bottles of good champagne, a tie, a scarf, chocolate, cologne, perfume, candles. The train is nearly empty.

"Are you going on Sunday?"

"I promised Mazin."

"Can we go together?"

She won't say, "Let's go together," or, "We're going together." She can't be that loose. Afraid that she'll be imposing, she maintains a slight sense of formality and caution.

"Obviously, we'll go together. Have you seen the address? Quai de la Tournelle. It'll be opulent."

"You think?"

"I do."

The *métro* stops at St. Paul and Mia collects her things. "O.K., I'll see you at graduation?"

I continue on, change to the four at Châtelet, get off at Odéon, cross Boulevard St. Germain, and walk down the rue de Seine. I pass Bar du Marché, full of people, mostly tourists, sitting on the terrace in the sun drinking expensive beer. I begin the long climb to my apartment—one hundred and seventy-seven steps. Today the stairs feel particularly steep, winding up and up, the bags heavy in my hands.

In a few hours the sun will spread a long rectangle of light across the floor. There's a large fireplace, a wide bed up a ladder in a mezzanine, a window that opens to the street.

The sun is low, the Eiffel Tower silhouetted against the sky to the west. I can see the golden cupola of l'Institut de France. To the south, the dark dome of the Palais du Luxembourg. Below, the cafés are crowded with people. Across the street, Pauline's window is open. Her boyfriend Sébastien stands shirtless washing dishes. A white Alsatian is stretched out in the sun fast asleep in front of Claude et Cie butchers. Down the rue de Buci, the little brown mutt keeps guard in front of the Café Conti and I stand in my window looking out, feeling the summer expanding in front of me. That familiar sense of freedom, a feeling inextricably linked to childhood, to having once been a student myself—released.

Pauline walks into the kitchen and kisses Séb on the shoulder. She sees me in my window, waves, and turns away to wrap her arms around his waist.

Watching them I imagine Isabelle, the two of us standing here looking out across the rooftops, the cold air slipping in, her back warm against my chest.

I used to think of her often. Washing dishes after dinner, I spoke to her. When it was cold and the heaters still weren't working I brought extra blankets to bed and pretended to hold her. In the evenings I came home to messages on the machine. Listening to her voice was like setting her free in the room. I made dinner and talked to her.

"Cut them thin," I said. "So thin they can't hold their own weight."

"I know, you've told me a thousand times."

"My mother cut onions like that."

But I never called her back.

She stopped leaving messages. Her voice was no longer there.

But there were still days when she appeared in front of me while I was standing at the window, and I could almost remember the way she smelled.

* * *

Sunday. On the street there are cool-eyed women everywhere. Bar du Marché is overflowing with people standing on the sidewalk waiting for tables. I cross Boulevard St. Germain at a jog, dodge a woman on a scooter. She smiles. I glide down the steps at Odéon and am on the *métro* in five minutes.

When I enter the gates of the school there are people milling around. Parents, grandparents, families from all over the world, all dressed for the day, summer dresses, hats, suits, video cameras. Walking through the crowd I hear French, Arabic, German, Korean, and Italian. But in the courtyard, and then in the foyer where people are waiting, it is mostly English, accented and punctuated with those other languages.

Just as I reach for a drink Mazin picks me up off the ground. "Dude."

"Dude," I say, "put me down."

Laughing, he drops me, steps back, and puts his hand to his chin as if inspecting a painting. "Nice threads."

"Damn right. Hands off."

"I need to go have my picture taken for, like, the millionth time with my brother but I'm going to see you tonight, right? Party *chez moi*."

"I'll be there, Maz."

He leans in, "Dude, did you see Carolina? *Dude*, girl is off the hook!"

I shake my head. "Mazin, go away."

* * *

That evening as Mia and I walked along the Quai de la Tournelle there was a strong wind blowing from the north.

We arrived at a perfectly maintained building. We could hear laughter from the balcony above us.

I entered the code and pushed open the heavy wooden door. As it closed behind us the street noise was gone and we stood in a wide courtyard. I'd walked past the building for years without a glance. And now, with a magic code, here was an immaculate courtyard. A neat rose garden. A purling fountain.

At the carved wooden doors I pressed an engraved silver button. A tall woman with long dark hair loose around her shoulders let us in—Mazin's mother. She wore a black satin dress and a wide hammered-gold bracelet on her wrist.

She kissed both of us and, although we'd never met, she knew who we were.

"Welcome. Welcome," she said, ushering us into the enormous apartment. In other rooms we could hear people talking, glasses clinking.

"You've both done so much for our boys. We're very happy to have you here. Please, have something to eat, some champagne."

The apartment was full of people—students, parents, friends and relatives. She led us down a wide hallway, which ran the length of the apartment. A bar had been set up against the wall and a serious-looking Frenchman in a tuxedo stood pouring champagne. When we got to the table he filled two delicate flutes with Krug and handed them to us.

The buzzer rang. "Please excuse me," Mazin's mother said. Across from us was a large dining room where a long table was spread with white tablecloths and platter after platter of Lebanese food. Beyond the tables were floor-to-ceiling windows, which opened to the terrace. Outside, there were people standing, talking, smoking, leaning over the railings, looking through the wide plane trees at the river below and out to the Île Saint Louis. On the bridge a man was tuning a guitar.

"Holy shit," Mia whispered and then Mazin, dressed in a suit too big for his thin frame and looking drunk, came into the dining room. His face brightened.

"Mr. S.! Ms. Keller!"

He kissed Mia and when I reached to shake his hand he gave me a look of pity, brushed my hand aside, and hugged me.

"Dude, you changed my life," he said. "We hug."

"Nice place you've got here," she said.

"It's ridiculous," he whispered. "Came with the move. Sort of embarrasses me so can we talk about something else please? Are you hungry? The food's awesome. It's all from Diwan. Do you know Diwan?"

From the buffet we could see a vast salon. A giant gilt-edged mirror hung above a fireplace. There were long sumptuous couches, a low glass table, and high ceilings laced with intricate moldings. The room was full of students. When they saw Mia and me some stiffened and hid their glasses, but most of them smiled or waved.

Mike Chandler was standing in the far corner of the living room with his elbow on the fireplace speaking in French with someone's father. Mia and I sat on two large leather chairs. I watched Mike, his gestures, his serious expression, his calm, the way he held his glass by the stem. None of it was contrived, none of it was the behavior of a teenager playing at adulthood. He'd been this way since birth.

These kids like Mike Chandler who were fluent in several languages and cultures, who were so relaxed, so natural in exquisite apartments at elaborate parties, who moved from country to country, from adult to adolescent with a professional ease, were not the standard at ISF.

Most were kids who'd been plucked from an Air Force base in Virginia and deposited in Paris, who resented the move, refused to adapt. The move only strengthened their faith in conservative American politics. They refused France. Their rebellion was, by default, an adamant rejection of their new home and all things French. Their families bought food from the commissary at the American Embassy. Kids who'd return from weekend

trips talked excitedly about the Taco Bell and Burger King they'd found at Ramstein.

Not these kids though, and as I looked around the room I felt proud of them for their apparent sophistication and also of myself for having become part of a world that was previously unknown to me.

Mazin's mother passed and tried to convince us to dance. We refused but on her second round she took Mia's hand and pulled her away.

Left alone, I finished eating, and then walked outside. Ariel Davis and Molly Gordon were leaning back against the railing.

"Hey Mr. Silver," Molly said.

Ariel smiled. I rested my elbows on the railing and looked out over the street.

"Big plans for the summer, Mr. Silver?" Molly asked.

"Going to Greece, you?"

"Staying here."

"I'm going to be in your seminar next year," Ariel said lighting a cigarette. She looked at me and ran her fingers through her black hair.

"Good," I said.

"So, you coming out with us tonight Mr. Silver?" Ariel asked looking down at the street.

"Out where?"

"We're going to Star and Stripe."

"We're all going," Molly said. "You should come. Bring Ms. Keller."

"Do you go out a lot, Mr. Silver?" Ariel asked.

"I'm out right now."

"Good point." She smiled at me again.

"Do you go to, like, bars?" Molly asked.

"No, usually I just stay home, drink tea, and read *The Canterbury Tales*."

22

"I know you totally go out," Ariel said laughing. "I saw you at Cab one night."

"Did you? I try to avoid bars full of Americans."

"Well you probably won't like Star very much then," Molly said.

The plane trees were creaking in the wind. Occasionally a couple passed beneath us. From time to time a taxi flew by, but otherwise all the noise of the evening was behind us in the apartment.

Ariel flicked her cigarette out in a long arc over the sidewalk below, where it landed in a burst of sparks. She looked directly at me and said, "Mr. Silver I hope you come tonight. It would be really fun to party with you. If not, I'll see you next year in seminar. I hear you're a great teacher."

I went in search of Mia.

On my way through the apartment I ran into Mazin's father, a handsome man in an expensive black suit. He shook my hand.

"Mr. Silver. I'm glad I found you. Mazin's been talking about you all year. I've been traveling so much. I'm sorry we're only meeting now. Do you have everything you need?"

I told him that I'd eaten, that the food was excellent, that he had a beautiful home.

"Listen, Mr. Silver, Mazin's never talked about a teacher the way he's talked about you. He's changed this year and I think it has a lot to do with your class. It is a difficult thing being away from your family, from your sons so much. It is the nature of my work of course. But nonetheless a difficult thing. The point is that I'm grateful to you."

"Thank you, sir. Your son is wonderful. He's grown up a lot this year. I've come to really care for him. You must be very proud."

"I am. We are."

I smiled.

"Another glass of champagne?"

"I'd better not."

"O.K., well, if there's anything I can ever do for you, Mr. Silver, please ask. As I said, I'm so grateful."

"This party is more than enough."

At the far end of the apartment, Mia was in a large room that had been turned into a dance floor. Glamorous, shoeless women danced, their arms reaching up toward the dimmed chandelier. A group of children, six or seven years old, wiggled around them. There were ISF students and graduates moving and singing with the music. Mia was there in the middle of a small group of girls, all of them thrilled by her presence.

I leaned against the wall and watched. From time to time one of the kids would pass by and try to get me to dance. I kept my place until Mazin's mother took me by the hand and pulled me onto the floor. It seemed as if everyone at the party was used to being there, that this was how it always was—family coming and going, people around.

The music sped up. Someone popped the cork from a bottle of champagne. Molly appeared, took my hands and pulled me across the room to a group of kids. Ariel tossed her hair. Mike Chandler, dancing behind her, winked at me as if he were my uncle, raised his glass and took a long drink. Ariel leaned back against him, grinned at me and closed her eyes.

Steven walked past and punched me on the shoulder.

"What up, Mr. S. Working it on the dance floor. Good to see, good to see."

Eventually I made my way through the crowd and back out onto the balcony. The night air felt good. I was giddy and didn't want to go home. I leaned out over the street. When Mia found me we watched the passing tourist boats for a while, their spotlights moving across the buildings, lighting us up while kids waved and shouted from the decks. Mia waved back. Neither of us spoke for a while. Then she touched my arm and took a long breath.

"William," she said. "William, William."

"It's beautiful. It's too much."

"Yes." I could feel her looking at me.

I closed my eyes.

"William," she said again. She was pressed against me, her hip to mine, her hand on my arm. I could smell her hair.

"So? Are we going out with them?" I asked.

I couldn't look at her.

I wanted to walk home alone along the river. Stop for a beer at La Palette. But it was all too beautiful to go home—the air, the rustling leaves slowly turning green to white, green to white, the water below, the sound of the guitar coming up off the bridge.

"Let's," she said. "We'll go for a drink."

Mia went to the bathroom. I put my coat on and waited in the living room. The apartment was still crowded. Ariel sat on the floor with a girl I recognized from school. They watched me and whispered until Ariel waved me over.

"So did you decide?" Ariel asked smiling, looking up at me.

"I think we're coming. I'm just waiting for Ms. Keller."

"Awesome. Oh, do you know Marie?"

"No," I said. "Hello, Marie."

"She's my best friend in the world." Ariel said, obviously drunk.

"Good to meet you. Maybe I'll see you both later."

"O.K., I'll see you," Marie said, raising her eyes to mine.

Waiting for Mia in front of the building, the wind was whipping the leaves around. It felt more like October than June. Looking up I could see people leaning over the balcony smoking cigarettes, their voices floating out. I was taken with the same kind of euphoria I'd felt repeatedly over the last few weeks—that sense of being precisely where I wanted to be, of having made it through. The wind rushing harder and harder up the river seemed to lift me and I was overcome with a sort of impatience that was only loosely connected to the night.

Someone on the balcony called down to me, "What up, Mr. S.? Shouldn't you be asleep, man? Little late for you."

I made an exaggerated bow and they laughed. Mia and a group of kids came out the door.

"Are you sure you want to do this?" I asked.

"It'll be fun. Anyway, I've told them we're going."

She turned to the group standing in front of the building.

"We'll see you there."

"Oh my God, you're coming, Silver?"

"Looks that way, Molly. Looks that way."

Mia and I caught a taxi. It had begun to rain. The driver flicked on the windshield wipers and turned up rue St. Jacques. I thought about getting out of the cab and walking home.

I closed my eyes and listened to the blades sweeping back and forth across the glass, the droning engine, the soft voice of the Radio Nova DJ.

Up the hill toward the Pantheon they were standing beneath a blue awning adorned with a single star.

"I'm not going in there," I whispered.

"Just walk."

Inside were stone stairs descending into the belly of the place, where it was crowded with students.

Mia and I found a place at the bar.

"It's mostly underclassmen here," she said, looking worried.

"I noticed that."

"It doesn't feel right. Maybe we should leave."

"Hey, you wanted to come and there's no way I'm leaving before I have a beer."

She looked around uncomfortably.

"Oh my God, I'm *so* buying you guys drinks." Molly, drunk and laughing, looked over our heads to catch the bartender's eye.

Leaning just past my ear, she called out, *"Henri! Trois Screaming Orgasms, trois."*

"This is so *cool*," she said giggling. "I can't believe I'm partying with you guys. It's totally, full on, surreal."

Mia, looking flushed, said, "I'm not sure this is the best idea, Molly."

"Ms. Keller, I graduated. I'm not even a student at the school. What's the big deal?" she asked reaching across the bar for the milky shots. With hers in hand, she said, "To the future." She smiled and raised her glass. "To all our futures. Totally."

* * *

The music got louder. Someone took my hand and pulled me onto the dance floor. We were packed tight. I began to dance, people passed in front of me, faces I recognized, shadows, light and dark and each student's face a subtle jolt, until they all became people in a bar.

I danced with Mia, and the drunker she became, the more determined she seemed to contain me. I spun away. Ariel appeared moving close, pressing her breasts against my chest, leaning her head back, smiling, turning away and returning.

I moved toward the bar where I drank a beer and watched the crowd.

I stood in the bathroom and pressed my head against the cold tile wall.

I pushed back onto the dance floor searching for Mia and found Ariel's friend. I couldn't remember her name. She smiled without hesitation, without artifice or experiment.

Marie.

She danced and I followed her into the center of the room, surrounded by what felt like thousands of people. She pushed tight against my cock, which hardened immediately. When she felt it against her, she pushed with more force, bent her knees and slowly, expertly glided her ass against me.

"Do you know who you're dancing with?" I asked.

She turned to face me, "Yes, Mr. Silver. Do you know who *you're* dancing with?"

I nodded.

"Congratulations," I said.

"For what?"

"Graduation. For graduating."

"Oh I didn't graduate, Mr. Silver. I'll be a senior next year. Same class as Ariel."

"Jesus Christ."

She took a step closer, pressing her breasts against me.

"It's your choice, Mr. Silver. I'll understand if you want to leave, I'll understand."

Her mouth was inches from mine.

"I have to leave," I said.

"O.K.," she smiled. "If you have to."

"Give me your number," she said into my ear. "Whisper it to me."

"No," I said.

"Whisper it to me, Mr. Silver. Whisper it to me, just in case."

* * *

Outside in the cold, early morning air I walked slowly along rue des Écoles until, as I knew it would, my phone rang.

"I'm meeting you," she said.

I stopped and sat on the hood of a parked car and waited. A drunken couple walked past, laughing, and I asked them for a cigarette. Blowing smoke into the cold air, I thought about leaving. I thought about going back to my apartment, ignoring the phone calls.

She came around the corner barefoot with her high heels in her hand. She had light green eyes and long auburn hair.

We walked in silence along the empty rue des Écoles. At Boulevard St. Michel, Marie ran barefoot against the light, laughing, leaving me waiting on the corner watching her on the other side, her arms outstretched, shoes dangling from her fingers.

"Come on," she yelled twirling on the pavement. "Come on."

After the traffic passed, I crossed the boulevard. "Come on," she said taking my arm. We were safer there where the streets were darker, hidden away behind l'École de Médecine, the cinemas closed for the night. Marie pulled my arm around her shoulders.

"I'm cold," she whispered.

I held her against me. At rue Antoine Dubois she pushed me against a wall and kissed me, her mouth perfectly warm. For a moment she was slow and languorous and then instantly on fire, her hand between my legs.

And then again she stopped. "Fuck," she said. "*Putain*! You're making me insane."

She broke away and walked to the steps behind the statue of Vulpian and sat down. I watched as she leaned back on her elbows, her bare feet on the cold stone. A couple came down the stairs from rue Monsieur le Prince. I stayed waiting in the shadows until they were gone. And then I went to her. She pulled me down onto the step and there was her warm mouth again.

"I can't," she said then. "Listen Mr. Silver, I'm really sorry but I can't do this now. It's not like I don't want to. Because I do. Every girl at school would kill to be in my position right now but this isn't a good time, O.K.? I've got my period and I just think that if we're going to do this we should do it, you know, when everything is, I don't know, *right*. You know what I mean?"

She looked at me, her lips smeared with red, and said that she'd better leave, that she'd better get back to her friends. Another time, she said. Another time we'd do this right. She'd show me what she was capable of. And how badly she wanted to. She stepped close, her breath smelling of the sweet gum she'd put in her mouth, and said, "Next year, Mr. Silver."

She left me on the steps. I watched her walk away. "Bye, Mr. Silver," she sang, waving with both hands and spinning in the street before she disappeared around the corner.

MARIE
25 YEARS OLD

I barely knew who the guy was. I mean, at the beginning of my junior year I don't think his name would have meant anything to me at all. Maybe his name. I'm not sure. The point is that I didn't know him. And more important is that I didn't care. There were those kids who were interested in teachers, who really cared or fell in love with them. They'd search for a math teacher on the web and find out she had a secret life or something. It's like they were amazed that a teacher might go home and take a shower, drink a beer, go to parties, fall in love. But I didn't care. Or maybe it was just that there was no mystery. I didn't get the surprise. Some of them you like. Some of them you don't. They were like our parents or our older sisters and brothers. They were like us, really. A lot like us if you think about it.

And some of those teachers? I mean they only spoke one language. Not even French. They'd never even lived in another country before France. And so many of us had lived in three, four, five different cities before Paris. And most of us spoke at least, at *least*, two languages. And flawlessly. So what did I care if some guy from Nebraska went home every night and got drunk?

We came to the same place every day. We all had our problems, our preferences, our talents, our failures. We were part of one another's lives.

My junior year I was miserable and lonely and tired and bored of everything. I wanted to get out of there. Out of ISF, out of Paris, out of France. Away.

I'd wake up at 5:45, have a coffee, maybe eat something, take a shower, and then stand in front of the mirror putting on lotion disgusted by my body trying to figure out what to wear. I dressed and hated my choice no matter what. I'd dry my hair, brush it, and put on makeup. Then afterward I'd call Ariel to make sure we weren't wearing the same thing.

When I went downstairs my mom would be in the kitchen, usually standing at the counter drinking her coffee. We'd barely speak. I'd say *bonjour, maman* and pretend to search for something in my backpack and if she spoke at all it was because she didn't like my shoes.

At 6:45 I'd leave and walk to the bus stop. We lived to the east, outside of Paris, near the school in St. Mandé in a nice house right up against a forest. From my window all I saw was green. My dad was the vice president of a company that made containers. Juice boxes, milk cartons, water bottles, yogurt cups.

The walk from the house was fifteen minutes and I'd spend the whole time on the phone with Ariel. She was my best friend. I hated her. That's one of the strange things about those years. You spend all your time with people you despise. Even after everything that happened with Colin, the way he treated me, the things he made me do, there's no question in my mind, I hated Ariel more. You can't imagine a hatred more intense, more pure. We were vicious. Not just us two. I mean all of those girls. I was right in the middle of it. I was *part* of it and looking back, remembering how mean we were, really hating one another, it still makes my stomach ache. You couldn't pay me enough money to go back to high school. Not as a teacher or a student or a visitor.

I caught the bus with all the other kids from my neighborhood, found a seat and tried to sleep or do some homework. I met Ariel by the front gate where we'd share a cigarette and tell each other how good we looked. She'd tell me her stories, I'd tell her mine, and then we'd go to class. That was it. When I wasn't in class I was with Colin or Ariel or both of them or some other people we were supposed to be friends with back then.

About Colin, I don't know what to say really. I can't remember a single conversation we had while we were together. I don't know what he said to me or what I said to him. Really the whole thing only matters at all because of what he did to me. I mean I remember it, him, because of that one thing. And maybe if that had never happened I wouldn't remember his face or what he smelled like.

GILAD

Our first day in Paris. We've been driven from Roissy to our new apartment on the rue de Tournon. My mom's in the living room, sitting on a low white couch facing the fireplace. All the windows are open. There's a slight smell of paint. My dad is in a light-brown linen suit he bought in Rome. A blue shirt. His pale orange tie draped over the back of the white chair in the corner. She's sitting with her arms spread out behind her. She's golden there, so tan, wearing a dress the color of his tie.

I sit in the chair facing my father. After so long in the desert, the absence of a buzzing air conditioner is loud. The street noise floats through. No one speaks. I look at her cheek. She's following my dad's gaze out the window. I'm sure I know what they're thinking.

This is the city where they fell in love. After all this time they've finally returned. All this time gone by. This marriage. It isn't happiness they feel. Something else. They feel possibility, a faint hope perhaps. But it has nothing to do with love. It has nothing to do with them together.

We're three people in a room.

We moved to Senegal when I was ten years old. My dad was the Counselor for Public Affairs at the American Embassy in Dakar. I went to school at ISD where I was taught to speak French by a Senegalese woman, one of the few locals employed as a teacher.

Because I was in love with her I learned to speak French. I

followed her everywhere and believed that we'd get married. I did whatever I could to be close to her and I listened carefully to everything she said. I'd never seen a woman like that. She spoke Senegalese French and taught us to speak like she did.

She wore a purple dress and smelled like garlic and onions. We cooked in her class and sang Senegalese songs. By the end of that year I spoke French well. I never exchanged an English word with Madame Mariama and when I left for the summer I cried in the car home.

She was fired when a group of parents complained that their children were speaking like the natives. Our new teacher was a pale Parisian ice cube. I refused to change my accent and I hated her. She hated me back.

That first summer in Paris I thought about Madame Mariama often. I loved speaking French. I got to know my neighborhood and found that I had more freedom there than anywhere I'd ever lived. We'd been in so many dangerous cities, behind so many gates in expatriate compounds, that arriving in Paris felt like being released from prison. It was the first time in my life that I didn't have a driver or a guard.

* * *

As the story goes, they fell in love here—my mom just out of college and beautiful. In the photographs she has long dark hair and dark skin. After graduating from Berkeley, she flew to Paris in 1980 and rented a little apartment. She wandered around with a leather-bound notebook. My grandparents had given her, as a graduation gift, an around-the-world plane ticket and some money. Paris should have been the beginning of a long series of adventures.

There's a photograph of her in black and white. She's sitting on the Pont Neuf with her head cocked to the side. She's wearing a thick turtleneck sweater, the sleeves drawn over her hands. She's wearing jeans and a beat-up old military coat.

The photograph is one of the few things I've kept. I study it for clues of her life before my father. There's a box of Gitanes beside her, a silver Zippo, a leather satchel at her feet. It's a great photograph, the light on her face, her closed eyes, the shadows, her lips just barely parted as if she were speaking to someone. She says she doesn't remember who took it. I don't believe her.

I imagine she's always dressed this way—big sweater, used coat. She's smoking cigarettes, sitting in the sun, men chasing her. She's full of ideas—places she'll go, paintings she'll paint, love she'll find. I can see her walking along the Seine with nowhere to be, a little money in her pocket but not too much. She's at bars, in cafés, one of those women who prefers men, who is loved by them, who flirts with strength rather than weakness. She's smiling at everyone and everyone is in awe of her or in love with her. The bartender, the butchers, the florists, the cheese man, the fishmonger, everyone in her neighborhood protects her, keeps an eye on her, hoping, with their protection, that she won't leave them, that she'll love them in return.

Beautiful Annabelle Lumen, twenty-two, smoker of French cigarettes, wanderer of the city, who loved art so much but had never entered Paris's greatest museum.

She'd waited, "preserving my virginity," she says, spending days sitting in the sun, eating her lunch, reading in the muted quiet of the Cour Carrée, listening to the musicians. She sat on the steps and sketched tourists. She waited until the weather got colder, until the tour buses were fewer. She waited for the winter to come and then, one cold day at the end of January, she walked from her apartment on the rue Montmartre into the grand courtyard, passed through the gleaming new glass pyramid and descended slowly into the dark center of the Louvre.

The story of how my parents' romance began is family legend. I've heard it told a thousand times. At embassy dinners and cocktail parties. It is a part of their public selves, part of their advertising.

It goes like this:

My father, Michael Fisher, straight out of Yale with a Master's in Economics, in Paris for a vacation before he flies to Africa for his first assignment at the US Embassy in Pretoria, looks away from Prud'hon's *The Empress Josephine* and sees my mother walking slowly across the gallery.

She is the first person to have passed in ten minutes and my father hears her footsteps before she appears. He glances at her and then returns to the painting. "It is as if," he says, "Josephine herself has wandered into the room."

Dad watches her. The way she's dressed, the ease with which she moves through the gallery, the way she swings her arms, all make him believe she's French. My father, a master of languages, has not then mastered French and wonders what to do.

"She is," he says to himself, "the most beautiful woman I have ever seen."

She terrifies him. And so rather than speaking to her, he takes from his wallet one of his fresh-cut business cards. On the back he writes: Do you speak English? He keeps the card in his hand and goes on pretending to admire Josephine. Then he gives himself an out: if she doesn't stop at this painting, he will let her leave undisturbed.

His heart beats. His palms sweat. She stops just behind him. He can feel her there. He can hear her pencil scratching across paper. He takes a breath. He counts to ten. He turns to her. He hands her the card, she looks at him surprised, thinks at first, she later says, that he's a missionary, a Jehovah's Witness, but accepts the card, reads his message, smiles, writes an answer on her half-finished sketch of Josephine, tears it from her notebook and gives it to him: Are you dumb?

He laughs aloud. His heart races. Seeing those words, that simple question, "Are you dumb?" written in her wild hand floating there where Prud'hon's dark woods should be, the story goes, "the world became a perfectly solvable equation."

And so he spoke.

"She's nearly as beautiful as you are," he says.

Suave Michael Fisher. The world a perfect proof.

"Do you think so?" my mother responds, gazing up at the painting, as if, my dad tells his guests, she were truly trying to decide who was more beautiful.

Finally she says, "You know, this Josephine, she had a pug named Fortune. She used him to send Napoleon secret messages. Did you know that?"

My father did not.

"On their wedding night Napoleon wouldn't let Fortune sleep with them and Josephine said, 'If the pug doesn't sleep in our bed neither do I.' You know what happened then?"

"They slept with the pug?"

"They slept with the pug."

"Smart man."

All this time Annabelle has been studying Josephine. Eventually, she turns to Michael, who's been studying Annabelle, and says, "I've got better teeth than she did. Did you know that she had famously awful teeth?"

What did she see when she finally looked at young Michael Fisher? A well-dressed man, wearing good shoes and a neat haircut. A man with gray eyes and a long, straight nose. Strong round shoulders. A wide, open, American face. Thick blond hair. An attractive, unremarkable looking man, whose flat eyes threw her—she couldn't tell if they were warm or cold.

Why she agreed to have a coffee with him in a café (neither of them can remember its name) on the Place Dauphine she wasn't sure. Certainly it wasn't the world falling into perfect order. She'd never describe love in those terms anyway, but whatever was propelling her away from a museum she'd waited nearly a year to visit, I promise it wasn't love.

And that's how they met—the museum, the café, and so on. Then they became inseparable. Lumen became Fisher. There's no detail after the café. We're to imagine the rest—the long walks through the city, the laughing, the glittering lights, an accordion, a rumbling *métro*, passion. People nod, they close their eyes. Ah Paris. Love. Romance. A chance meeting. But what is it they imagine, these guests of my parents who nod and smile, enraptured by my impeccably dressed father and his charming story? What do they see? What is it that happens next? Why does my mother stay with him? Why does she pack up her apartment on the rue Montmartre with her flower boxes in the window? What makes her move to Africa with this man she's known only two weeks? This man who has so little art in him.

But nobody seems interested in the answers to these questions. No one seems compelled even to ask. It's all simply understood—the lovely couple, the brilliant young man, the beautiful young woman, one day in the Louvre.

And I can understand leaving with him—the clean entry into a place she'd never been, the exotic idea of Africa, the spontaneity of it. The pleasure of the phone call home, "I met a man. I'm moving to Pretoria." Oh, our reckless daughter. But why did she stay? Why did she let herself get pregnant? Why did she follow him around the world for so long?

* * *

August came. I loved my new city. I went everywhere. I found the Goutte d'Or, hidden down the hill from Sacré-Coeur, a village really. Little Africa. I wandered those streets day after day

44

feeling nostalgic for Senegal. The markets swarmed with people wearing leather sandals and *boubous*. There were makeshift mosques, small restaurants serving cheap bowls of *Thiébou Dien*.

I didn't have a single friend that summer but I don't remember ever feeling lonely. It was a kind of religious experience. I felt, for the first time in my life, a new sense of possibility, hope even, and belonging. That summer I was, I'm sure, as happy as I'd ever been.

The emptiness of Paris in August allowed me a new sense of ownership, of possession. There was a laziness about the city without traffic. So little noise. More and more I moved through the streets, sliding in and out of *métros*, fluidly transferring from train to train, bus to bus. I rarely used my map. I invented games for myself where each decision I made about where to go was determined by a flip of a coin. A bus would pass. Heads yes. Tails no.

I'd never had many friends in other cities, but there had always been people around. The compounds where we lived— heavily guarded, walled neighborhoods—forced us to interact. There'd always be a pool. There were always parties, somebody's mother serving lemonade, somebody's father grilling chicken breasts.

There was nowhere to go. You couldn't leave without your driver and, in some places, without your driver and bodyguard. If you want to see the city you're living in you do it through the bulletproof glass of your car. When we did go out shopping in local markets or to restaurants or museums, we were made so conspicuous by our attendants that I only wanted to leave. I always hated the spectacle we made. We were isolated in the countries we lived in. It was like living in a wealthy, American suburb—nice homes, swimming pools, maids, alarm systems, and so on. The friends I had were just kids who were around. Kids from school, kids who lived next door, kids from the neighborhood and somewhere I lost interest.

It wasn't until Paris that something shifted. Paris was the beginning. Paris was everything.

August passed slowly. And then there was school.

MARIE

On the weekends I'd usually sleep at Ariel's because she lived in Paris and her parents were never around. Her apartment was in the sixteenth on the rue La Pérouse right near the Kléber *métro*. On Fridays I'd bring an extra bag and we'd go straight there after school. Maybe we'd go shopping before or see a movie on the Champs-Élysées. Otherwise we'd just sit around talking and eating, doing our homework and smoking our cigarettes out the window.

We'd get a little drunk on vodka and Coke and get dressed. My whole high school life starts to feel like an endless dressing room. Always standing in front of mirrors, checking my breasts, putting on makeup, turning around to look at my ass.

I hated the way I looked when I was alone and I hated myself more when I was next to Ariel, who was beautiful. I mean that she was really beautiful. It's a fact. I don't exaggerate about things like this. She had long black hair and perfect pale skin and a great body and bright blue eyes. She was so beautiful it was boring.

We'd stand in front of her mirror together trying on outfits, taking things off, putting things on, drinking our vodka and Cokes. It was her drink by the way. I only drank it because she'd decided that's what we'd do. She'd tell me how pretty I was, how she envied my body. I'd tell her she was crazy, that I wished I had hers. The whole thing was such bullshit. But that's your life then. Really that's the most terrible thing about it.

Anyway, I know how attractive I am. I mean to what degree

I'm attractive. I knew then too. I'm not spectacular and then in high school I was pretty much the same. I had a body that other people liked but it wasn't the one I wanted. It wasn't the one I thought was most appealing. I had nice breasts. That's true. But they embarrassed me and I didn't really want them then. I thought they weren't subtle. They weren't elegant. They weren't Parisian enough. Even if my mother is French, and they're basically just her breasts, they still didn't look right to me.

Then there was Ariel in her long thin body telling me about how she wished she had *my* body. And what's worse she was American. Both my parents are French and even if we spent all that time in New York, I was still French. I thought I should have looked it. And my mother thought the same thing. If you've never had a French mother you can't understand what she expected of me when it came to my appearance, to style. To be fair, I should say a Parisian mother. A Parisian mother with money. And I'm not talking about my father's money. I mean money. I mean that my mother was born and raised in Paris with money. In the seventh. She still wears the fucking *chevalière*.

She thought New York ruined me, made me American. Made me clunky, round, big. American. In all senses. The way I spoke English with an American accent, the way I spoke French with an American accent. She thought I did everything with an American accent.

Anyway, if Ariel wanted my big breasts it was true only because boys looked at me the way boys look at you when you have breasts like mine. She insisted that I wear tight low-cut tops when we went out. She said I was crazy to waste my body hiding it. I felt like an idiot at first but it wouldn't be true to say that I didn't like the attention. Still, without her I'd never have worn those clothes.

We'd go to Cab or VIP or a bar in the Latin quarter. Ariel preferred the clubs so we went there more often. The guys were older, better dressed, wealthier, more attractive, more European, there were fewer expats. They'd buy us drinks. Whatever we wanted. They wouldn't leave us alone. Ariel loved it. I don't know how many times I went back to her apartment by myself.

No one had any idea how old we were. There were men there as old as our fathers. But most of them were twenty-five, thirty. All she had to do was smile from our table. She was fearless. I'll give her that. You've never seen someone so happy. To tell the truth she was dazzling those nights. Men were just drawn to her. Not that they didn't talk to me. Of course. We were two young girls in a nightclub. But God they loved her and she would just light up. And the more they looked the more she'd glow. She wouldn't talk to the boys our age. She just wasn't interested. She said the weekends were for men. School was for boys.

Sometimes she came home when it was still dark. But just as often it was eight or nine the next morning. If her parents were around she'd call me to make sure they were asleep. Sometimes I'd distract her dad in the kitchen, ask for his help with something, so that she could get in without being noticed. I don't think they'd have cared anyway. They were those kind of parents. Ariel liked to pretend they were watching over her, but we both knew that was bullshit.

The closest I ever felt to her was those mornings. We lay in bed and I listened to her stories. She told me about the guy's apartment, his car, how terrible he was in bed, how fast he came, his bizarre fantasies. We giggled and I listened, trying to imagine Ariel's strange secret life. She tried to convince me to do it too. Just choose one of them and do it, she said. For a while I thought I would. There were some very beautiful, very glamorous people in those places. But whenever it came down to it I couldn't. I don't know why. I preferred waiting for her in bed.

By the end of the year I was exhausted. I was too thin. I drank too much. I felt like a zombie. I'd get home late. I'd do my homework and talk on the phone. Then at eight I'd come down for dinner. When my dad wasn't in New York or traveling somewhere else he'd be there, just getting home, still wearing his suit. I liked those dinners when it was the three of us. And during her holidays my sister would be there too. That's when things were the best. She'd been at NYU for three years and I still felt like she'd left a black hole behind her, like there was this massive absence, that we'd all been left floating in space. Even though we'd never been very close, her leaving changed the balance. My dad saw her all the time in New York. They'd have dinner together at good restaurants. He took her to the ballet. It drove me crazy with jealousy. But it was nothing compared to what it did to my mother.

After dinner I'd go to my room and work until I couldn't keep my eyes open. Then I'd get into bed and call Ariel. We'd talk until one of us fell asleep. In the morning I'd get up and do it again. By June I had nothing left. I felt completely strung out and after the year was over and after Colin, all I wanted was for school to end and to be free of that place.

* * *

I went with Ariel to a party for the graduating seniors. That's where I met him. I mean by that point I knew who he was. I'd seen him around. Girls talked about him. He was good looking but it's not like he was the most beautiful man I'd ever seen. Not at all. He wasn't really my type I don't think. I mean if I even *had* a type then. He wasn't very tall. Still, he had nice eyes and it's true there was something about him. And Ariel liked him. He was famous at school. He was a perfect target for her. When I met him I was very drunk. It's not as if I had plans. I didn't even think about it. When we left the party everyone went out and I just went along. I followed Ariel like always. When we got there she ordered us our drinks and we started to dance.

The funny thing is that I liked being there because there were so many kids. I remember thinking, this is nice, this is good. I was relieved. I felt safe.

Ariel saw him first. He was there with Ms. Keller. Just the two of them. They seemed happy. I mean like it was natural. They were at ease, they laughed. They seemed to really like each other. I watched for a long time. I didn't know them then but the way they were talking, the way they smiled, I don't know, they just seemed good together. And not as if they were in love, just that they seemed like real people. Sure of themselves. Solid. Adults. Good adults. Like they were what I wanted to be.

I had this quick waking fantasy. You know the way you do when you're watching people on the *métro* and you imagine their lives. It was like that. I remember I was standing there watching them, pretending we were all at a restaurant together just the three of us talking like they were doing, laughing and feeling calm like they seemed. I don't know. I was pretty drunk by then.

But Ariel thought I was staring at him. And she whispered, You like him don't you? You should try to fuck him tonight. She destroyed everything. I remember thinking how I never wanted to see her again. How it wasn't only ISF and Paris and France that I wanted to escape from but it was Ariel too. And it made me so sad. Not just Ariel but all of it.

Anyway, I laughed and told her I had to go to the bathroom. O.K. let's go, she said, because it was impossible then for us to go alone. So I shut myself in the stall and pretended to pee. I sat on the toilet seat staring at the tiles on the floor while she looked at her face in the mirror, and I swear to God I never felt more lonely than in those few minutes in that fucking bathroom.

I could have stayed in there the rest of the night listening to the music through the walls but Ariel was impatient. When I came out she was putting on eyeliner. She said it was our one chance, how maybe we'd never see him out at a bar like this again. Maybe we should take him home together, she said laughing and looking at me in the mirror, raising her eyebrows. I shook my head but she kept talking about it. I'd go down on you for him, she said and started to laugh.

Ariel loved to talk but I think then she was serious. I'm sure she would have. For him. For the performance. Who could resist the two of us? she asked. She was dancing in front of the mirror looking at herself. I wanted to slap her. Well if you're not interested, she said, I'll do it myself.

He's a fucking teacher, I said.

Exactly, Marie. Exactly.

When we came out of the bathroom it seemed even more crowded. We could barely move. Somehow Ariel got us more drinks and we drank them fast. God I was drunk. I let myself get bounced around hoping the crowd would take me away from her. And it did and then I saw him and not really knowing why I sort of floated over to him. Then there we were the two of us like that. At first I don't think he had any idea who I was. He smiled at me. The first thing I thought was, he seems happy, like he's having a good time. And that was nice. Most people at those places never seem like they're having a good time. We danced close right away. There wasn't much choice. He looked right at me. He made me nervous but he wasn't creepy. I don't remember what we talked about. I tried to be witty. Anyway, it was loud and hard to hear and mostly we just danced close and I felt protected by the crowd and sort of crushed in there with him as if we were under a blanket together or something.

I kept thinking about how he was looking at me. I mean he

was this man, you know? It was surprising. It shouldn't have been, and looking back it's obviously not surprising at all. But at the time I was amazed. God, the way he was looking at me. He looked only at me and I just couldn't get over it, that he saw me that way. It was jarring and I suddenly felt as if I'd been thrown into this new world, and it was scary and exciting and strange and most of all it was shocking, just completely shocking, that this man, this adult person, was looking at me in that way. I don't know why I allowed it to be him, after all those nights out with Ariel.

Again, there's nothing surprising about it now. Of course. But then, then I was just blown away and I felt like in those few minutes, everything, everything had shifted. And at some point we started to touch and I felt him get hard against me. I was terrified. I was excited but I was terrified. I mean terrified to the point that I thought I might throw up. I turned around because I didn't want him to see me get sick if I was going to get sick. And I felt him there behind me and he was so hard and there was this moment when I really felt like I was going to run, you know those few seconds when you're not sure if you're going to be sick, and I just kept dancing and pushing back against him waiting for my body to figure out what the hell it was going to do and I waited, stuck there, so afraid. I was cold and my palms were sweating. I looked up and saw Ariel sort of smiling at me, but not really. She raised her eyebrows like she was encouraging me but I could tell she was angry and then she disappeared behind someone and I felt better all of a sudden and I knew that I wasn't going to throw up. I was warm again and I closed my eyes and just fell into him.

He was nervous, I could tell, and said he had to leave. But he gave me his number and he knew I'd call him. He must have. And I did.

I got out of there and I found him waiting for me on the hood of a car smoking a cigarette. He looked so calm, so sure of himself sitting on that fucking car.

We ended up on some steps in the dark. It was cold and I kept falling into him and I was so happy. It was strange. I mean I was elated. He kissed me so softly. I mean no one had ever kissed me like that. No one had even come close to kissing me like that. Not even in the same world. There was no rush. His mouth soft and warm and my God he was gentle. And that's what got me. That's what got me. He was tender. I mean truly tender. At that time, at that moment in my life, I mean Christ. It was over. The way he touched me, it made me want to cry. I don't know how else to say it: I was completely overwhelmed. I could barely breathe and I kept jumping around like an idiot, like a kid and he sat there smiling at me, his serene little smile like he knew everything, everything. And I was dancing around—I think I had my shoes off—and he was sitting there looking at me with that smile and those eyes and I had to get out of there. So I told him I had my period. I don't know why I told him that, why I didn't just go home with him.

That was it. He kissed me again and my heart was pounding, pounding. I had to get out of there.

I went to Ariel's. It was late. I took a taxi. She was in bed and I crawled in and told her everything. I knew she was furious. I rolled onto my side, smiled into the dark and fell asleep.

WILL

I spent the summer in Santorini. Each morning I woke in my small room and ate breakfast on the terrace overlooking the sea. I'd smile at the old woman who served me, walk out to the pool, find a chair, and read in the sun. In the afternoons I'd sit in a taverna on the water and eat fava and grilled octopus and drink beer. Afterward, I'd sleep, read, and watch the kids diving from the rocks. Later I'd go for a run high above the town along the ridge and toward Imerovigli. On the way back I'd stop at the rose church and sit on the wall and watch the sunset. Often, a white dog, thin and wolf-like, would run with me and then sit at my side panting as the sun fell.

Once there was a woman leaning against the wall, her face pretty in the orange light. We stood together, the two of us and the dog, and though I wanted to, I didn't speak to her.

The sun fell lower and lower, the wind came up, the sweat on my skin began to dry. Eventually, she left, nodding at me, smiling shyly and I watched her walk slowly down the path toward town.

Except for the few words of Greek I spoke to the sweet woman who brought my breakfast, I'd barely spoken to anyone since leaving Paris.

Good morning.

How are you?

Thank you.

A beer at the bar in town. Dinner too. I made no effort to meet anyone. I never approached the women who looked at me. After dinner I sat on the wall of the old fort and rolled cigarettes, smoked them and watched the moon rise. I listened to conversations, lovers whispering together, hidden away beneath the castle walls.

Sometimes in the evening I'd say something out loud just to remind myself that I was there, that I was capable of language.

"Jump," I'd say.

Or, "Telephone."

Or, "Isabelle."

Lying in my bed staring up at the ceiling I'd listen to those words floating around the room.

A few days before I left, I walked down to Amoudi Bay past the donkeys transporting other tourists up the steep path back to Oia. I walked past the tavernas and around the high rocks above the water. It was late in the afternoon, the wind had come up, and the small beach was nearly deserted. I spread my towel out over a flat rock and stood on the edge looking down over the water.

I felt the air warm and soft. I dove out and fell down into the cool water, breaking through the surface, suddenly surrounded, deeper and deeper. I stayed down as long as I could, waiting until I needed to return. And bursting through there was an intense jolt of joy, as if only here, in the water, with the warm wind and the taste of salt in my mouth, could I feel, could I shake my memory clear, shock away the familiar numbness. I put my head down and swam hard for the small island and its chapel built into the rock. I lay pressing my chest, my legs, stomach, palms, face against the hot stone, water pooling around me, warming in the sun. The water dried leaving a thin layer of salt tightening my skin as if the sky itself was pushing against me. The sky, the water, the warmth, the wind, the stone beneath me, I wanted to keep it, fold myself into it. Or it into myself.

* * *

I packed my small bag. The old woman from the hotel put her hands on my shoulders and said something I did not understand. I climbed into a taxi and waved to her. She stood with one hand on her hip, the other moving back and forth through the morning air.

Sitting in the airport, waiting for my flight to Paris, I thought of her round cheeks, thick hands, her black skirts, the sympathetic looks each morning as she brought me extra honey, her sad, encouraging good-bye. I looked down as we arced out over the island, the sea below a plate of blue, the sun just rising over the water. She'd pitied me.

GILAD

The school buses looked like those you see parked in front of Trocadero belching tourists onto the esplanade. Big things with comfortable, reclining seats. A whole fleet of them. The school invented bus stops, certain corners in each *arrondissement* where you'd get picked up. The first day of school there were nervous parents throughout the city standing on the sidewalk holding their children's hands waiting for the buses to arrive.

I waited alone that first morning, so sure of myself, and when the bus came I climbed on to find it packed with Americans. Why that surprised me I can't imagine. It had always been the same everywhere I'd been. I'd spent so much time on my own in the city, communicating in French, that I'd forgotten where I'd be going to school.

Usually it was straight directly from the airport to the compound, to embassy welcomes, to neighborhood parties, to school orientations. There had never been a time to forget that you were foreign, that you'd be driven around, kept apart. So the shock of climbing onto that bus and seeing the kids dressed as they were, speaking as they did, was terrible.

There were baseball hats turned backward, Knicks jerseys, and so on. The usual American shit. I found a seat and leaned my head against the window and listened to the same conversations.

Where are you from? Where did you live before this? Do you speak French? Do you like it here? Do you know John?

Did you know Kelly? How was your summer? Have you seen Julia? Ben looks so hot. On and on.

It made me tired. It was worse here as we passed through the city, stopping to collect more along the way. I wanted nothing to do with it. I wanted to find more of Paris, to make Parisian friends, to escape from this world. For the first time in my life, I was sure I could become a local, could be swallowed up by a place, could move unnoticed through the streets and this, this international school, this bus, was yet another American badge.

There was a black metal gate that ran the length of the school's property. We turned into the parking lot and followed a line of other buses as they pulled up along the curb to let students out.

You'd think that the International School of France would be a collection of beautiful buildings, ivy, lawns, and a Gothic bell tower maybe. Something academic, regal, scholarly. I imagined something traditional, something elegant.

The school reminded me of visa-processing offices, of vaccination centers in Africa, of aging hospitals. It felt like bureaucracy and routine. Having attended so many of these schools, I was used to the sudden rush of kids speaking English in their American uniforms—Gap, Banana Republic, Nike, Abercrombie and Fitch, and so on.

I'd been so sure that this school would be something beautiful.

There was a tall man with a silver ponytail and glasses standing in the foyer loudly directing traffic.

"Please move down the hall to the auditorium. Don't worry about finding your lockers, just move down the hall, find a seat and sit in it."

He wore a rumpled suit and waved his hands as if sending airplanes to their hangars.

"Please do not stop at your lockers. Go directly to the auditorium. What did I just say, what did I *just* say?"

In the auditorium a few hundred cramped seats descended to a large stage. I found an empty place on an aisle. The kids who knew one another talked about their summers, gossiped, scanned the crowd for familiar faces, people to smile at, people to hate, and so on. The same scene everywhere. First day of school, the usual gossip, the usual team making.

"Please, everyone sit down. This won't take long. Please. Quiet. Everyone. Everyone."

It's a universal language that headmasters, school directors, and principals speak. Whatever the title, you hear the same cadence, the same rhythms, the same techniques. Everyone. Beat. Everyone. It has to be a learned code. A sort of prayer to quietness. And amazingly, the room quiets.

"My name is Paul Spencer. I'm the head of the upper school. I know many of you and quite a few of you I don't know."

"What up, Spence?" someone yelled from the back of the auditorium.

Mr. Spencer smiled. "Clearly some of you are enthusiastic about the new school year. That's good. Indeed, while my name is Mr. Spencer, I'm popularly known as Spence. You're welcome to call me either."

Spence continued. We were welcomed, encouraged, informed, welcomed and encouraged once more and then released into our day. There was nothing about France in his speech. Nothing about the city and its relationship to the school or how lucky we were to be there, or what an honor it was to be studying in a city like Paris. There was nothing in his introduction about how Paris would be an integral part of our education, about the way that art and culture and language and food would be incorporated into our daily experience at the International School of France. And that's what I remember most from that first morning—the mundane nature of the experience and how the city I'd fallen in love with had been totally ignored. The city was irrelevant to the school.

ISF was its own country.

* * *

After the speech we had twenty minutes to find our lockers and make sure that the combinations we'd been given worked with the built-in locks. I found mine, number 225. I stared into it for a moment, reached into my backpack, took out several pens and placed them on the bottom of the locker. I took long breaths not knowing what to do. I kept my right hand on the door and moved it on its hinge—open and closed, open and closed. I don't remember how long I was there but eventually I turned and walked away. I didn't know the school at all but you walk as if you do. I wanted to get outside. Already they were looking at me. He doesn't talk to anyone. He just stares into his locker.

I walked out onto the field behind the school, a wide green lawn running the length of the building and edged by tall poplar trees. Beyond the field toward the school cafeteria were some picnic benches.

One of them was set to the side beneath a small pine tree. I sat there looking back at the school, a strong wind blowing the poplars from side to side. I liked those trees and the way they moved so slowly. I sat at the table until I heard the bell ring—a strange electronic reproduction of a church bell.

* * *

He was wearing jeans and a white shirt, his hair dark and cut short. The desks were arranged in a circle with his at the front of the classroom. He was sitting on its edge, holding one of those classic teacher's grade books—dark green and spiral bound.

The lights were off. The curtains had been pulled back and the windows were open as wide as they'd go. Through them I could see the swaying poplars.

He glanced up at me and smiled when I walked in.

He had striking green eyes and very long eyelashes, which made him look feminine. He had a few days' stubble and was very tan. His jaw was square but he had round boyish cheeks. Each of his physical features seemed to contrast another. I couldn't tell what he was—old or young, tall or short, sharp or soft.

I paused at a desk beneath one of the windows.

"Excuse me," I said. "Can I sit where I want?"

"Sure. Wherever you'd like. What's your name?" he asked me.

I told him. He nodded marking something in his grade book.

"I'm Mr. Silver."

Other students began to trickle in. He smiled at the ones who acknowledged him and ignored the ones who didn't.

He continued to write in his grade book until there were ten of us there. Nobody spoke. Nobody seemed to know anyone else. The bell rang. He kept writing. He made us wait. Then he looked up and read our names from his book. After each of our names he smiled or nodded or said hello.

Then, after he'd finished, he pushed himself off his desk and stood.

"So, welcome to Senior Seminar. For those of you who don't know me, and it looks as if we have a lot of new students here, my name is Mr. Silver. Two facts are important: you're all seniors. You have elected to be here.

"I'll assume that you will be responsible, engaged, active, and enthusiastic members of this group. We will meet here every morning for approximately one hour, four days a week for nine months. That's a lot of time. It is also no time at all.

"I will not, as I do for my tenth graders, give you a list of rules and expectations. I have no papers for you. No list of supplies. What you need to know is not complicated.

"As I mentioned before, the class is a seminar. I take this seriously. We will sit here every day and discuss literature. What that means will be up to you. I gauge the success of our class by the amount of talking I do. If I'm compelled to speak often then I will consider the class a failure. If I speak little then it is a success.

"Your own success will be based on three factors—the quality of your participation, the quality of your writing, and your enthusiasm for both.

"I would like not to give quizzes or tests of any kind. If, however, I believe that you're not reading what I ask you to read I will provide you with the kind of tests I give to my younger students. I will begin the year by treating each of you as adults. This means that you may use whatever language you like. You may express whatever opinions you have. You may refer to your personal experience. As long as you demonstrate an enthusiasm for the work we're doing here you're free to express yourselves as you wish.

"There are several exceptions. I will not tolerate cruelty to or disrespect of other students. I will not tolerate bigotry. I will not tolerate rudeness, bullying, or violence of any kind. Outside of those restrictions, you're free. Freedom. A problem we'll talk about in more depth later. What you say in this room will remain here. I will not discuss what you say with anyone else—not your parents, not other students, not faculty.

"Again, there are exceptions. If you indicate that you're planning to harm yourself or someone else I will not keep that information private. If you indicate that you're a victim of abuse I will not keep that information private. If you indicate that you have broken the law or plan to break the law I may not keep that information private.

"Outside of these exceptions you have my word that I will keep your secrets.

"I will expect you to arrive in class prepared, having done the work I've asked you to do. I take for granted that you are intelligent men and women capable of independent thought and that you are here because you want to be. Why you want to be here is a question we'll deal with later in the year but I absolutely do not accept the notion that you're here against your will."

A slight, compact, red haired kid raised his hand.

Mr. Silver coolly looked him in the eye until he put his hand down.

"I will answer any questions you have at the end of class. I'd like to finish first. Ideally we will arrive here each morning and forget, for an hour, that there is a world outside the classroom. However, I've been teaching long enough to know that this will not always be the case. The world will enter the classroom. You'll become angry with me. You'll disagree. You'll be bored. You'll be infuriated. And I may be as well. I expect all of that. But at least now you know my dream."

He smiled.

"To arrive here excited. That's what I want, for all of us to arrive here excited and to spend our time together happily challenging one another, to think, to push ourselves, to do beautiful work.

"In the first week I'll introduce existentialism and so will talk more than usual. Then we'll read Jean-Paul Sartre's famous lecture in which he explains and defends existentialism against its critics—something I'll have to do myself as many of you will yourselves become critics of existentialism. Or at least, I hope so.

"I will depend upon your ability to be critical, sharp, and

alert. I will make mistakes. I will say things that are not true. I will make arguments that are unsound. I expect that you will correct me. I expect that you will challenge me, question my logic, and consider my assertions critically.

"So, I have ten copies here of Sartre's lecture *Existentialism is a Humanism*. This will be our first text. For those of you who read French I encourage you to read it in the original too. All of you need to read this translated edition by Monday. The first fifty pages should be finished by Thursday.

"Let me end by saying this. Fling yourself into it headfirst. Everything can change, but only with abandon."

I wrote that down. It was the first note I took. I had one of those black and white marbled composition books. Brand new. I wrote in black pen across the first page, "Everything can change but only with abandon."

He took the stack of books from his desk and moved slowly through the room handing them out. We were quiet. I'm embarrassed to say it but I had chills.

I watched him—the way he placed the books on our desks, the way he moved through the room, and then the way the girls looked at him. From the beginning I envied him.

"Are there questions?" he asked.

The curly-haired guy on the other side of the room raised his hand again.

"What's your name?"

"Colin White," he said in a heavy Dublin accent. "Sir, you said we have a choice to be here but I didn't sign up for this. They just put me here."

Mr. Silver nodded slowly and said, "They just put you here."

WILL

It's always good at the beginning. You get over the shock of waking up early. You settle into the routine. You're grateful to be out with the street cleaners. It feels good in the cool morning. You're one of the first at the boulangerie, the *pain aux raisins* is still warm. Once you drag yourself out of bed, it's good to be back.

All the plans you have. The changes you'll make. You're fresh, you're brimming with enthusiasm, you're like the kids with their new notebooks, their promises to be better.

Each September we all make the same promises.

You stand before your classes and tell them what you want. You speak seriously, earnestly, and you believe in what you're saying. Or I did. It's September and the year is just beginning.

If you're soft at the start you'll drown. So you charm them by being tough, by staring down the talkers, by cutting down the challengers. You give them responsibility and freedom. You show them that you care, that you love what you do. You show them that you love the books, the ideas, learning, philosophy, something. You wonder if the pleasure you feel upon returning to school lies exclusively in the performing, in being adored. You wonder if teaching, the kind of teaching you do, is just celebrity making. You know your audience. You know what you can do. You can't help yourself.

You always begin the same way. You're standing on stage presenting yourself, happy to be back. Which is not to say that you don't believe in teaching, because you do. There are few things you believe in more and you want to do something good. But along with that comes the wonder of standing before a group of people who love you, who imagine that you are strong and wise.

All that attention, it's hard to resist. And if you're honest you acknowledge that before you ever became a teacher you imagined your students' reverence, your ability to seduce, the stories you'd tell, the wisdom you'd impart. You know that teaching is the combination of theater and love, ego and belief. You know that the subject you teach isn't nearly as important as how you use it.

* * *

It was my third year teaching at ISF, my tenth as a teacher. I was thirty-three years old.

I had four classes—three sections of tenth grade English— *Huckleberry Finn, Macbeth, The Grapes of Wrath, Civil Disobedience*—and one section of Senior Seminar. The class would be, I imagined then, a haven from the repetition of teaching sophomores the difference between Transcendentalism and Romanticism, explaining why Macbeth "talks like that," trying to convince my students that Thoreau had something to do with their lives.

Not that I didn't like teaching tenth grade. But the curriculum was the same year after year. I was tired of listening to myself talk. I was tired of the road-weary Joads, of Blake, of Whitman. I never tired of *Macbeth* but the fatigue I felt in teaching that class worried me. I focused my energy on my seminar.

In Greece I had read Sartre for the first time. I ran along the cliffs. I returned to my hotel room dripping with sweat to scribble my plans for the class in a notebook. Field trips and essay topics. It was the first course I'd been able to create from scratch without the influence of an English department.

I believed that this seminar would buoy me, would carry me through my third year at ISF. I'd teach with everything I had, devote myself to it, assign difficult work, learn along with my students, teach as if I were a first year teacher. I would, for the first time since I'd begun at ISF, come to class committed. That is, without plans for escape, for a new career, without the idea of teaching the needy in some unspecified African nation, living cheap in Thailand or any of the other fantasies I used to avoid the apparent permanence of my present life.

GILAD

I see their faces, their backpacks, their clothes, their note-books.

Cara Lee, a quiet, brooding Korean girl who sat across the room from me. Ariel Davis, a strange, aloof, deadly sexy girl with long black hair. Jane Woodhouse who once wore angel wings to class and began all of her statements with "I don't know what I'm trying to say here." Abdul Al Mady, nervous and painfully awkward. Hala Bedawi, a graceful and smiling brilliant Lebanese girl who understood things twenty minutes before anyone else. Colin White, a tough, wiry, kid from Dublin who seemed totally out of place at ISF, who carried with him a suppressed violence I'd never seen in expensive international schools. Aldo something, who sat as close as he could to Ariel and always agreed with her. She abused him, bestowing and withdrawing attention as her moods dictated. Rick Tompkins, a strong, cocky soccer player. And there was pretty Lily Brevet with her braids and heavy breasts.

One day early that year he drew a black swirl of lines on the board. I copied it into my notebook, a notebook I still have. I recorded everything I could those months. I imagined I'd make a movie, the camera moving from the trees across the field and gliding into the room. Mr. Silver at his desk. And then he looks up. And then he begins.

I listened. I sketched us. Day after day I wrote dialogue and now it serves as an intricate map.

On the first page there is this:

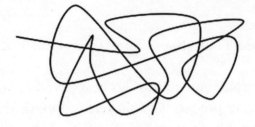

What is.

Then beneath that drawing a few inches down the page I have the same drawing but this time with a grid superimposed on top of it:

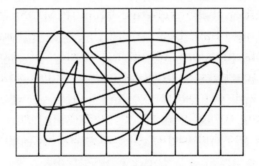

What we insist it is.

"Existentialists, more or less, believe that the human world is like this," he said, pointing to the scribble. "What does Sartre say about the letter opener?"

It was the first time he'd asked a direct question to the class. I don't remember if I knew what Sartre had said about the letter opener but I know that I didn't answer the question.

Colin White raised his hand.

"It's Colin, right?"

"Yes sir."

"Two things before you answer my question—first, you don't need to raise your hand and second, please don't call me sir. It's creepy."

We laughed.

"Sartre doesn't talk about a letter opener, sir, he talks about a paper knife."

Mr. Silver smiled and nodded his head, "You're right, Colin. Thanks for being precise. You do realize though that they're two names for the same thing?"

"I do, sir."

"So why make the point?"

"You asked us to correct you, sir."

"Indeed I did. I also asked you not to call me sir and yet you've done so three times since I made that request."

"It's habit, sir. Sorry."

I remember their exchange because Mr. Silver indulged Colin. It would have been so much easier to brush him off, to ignore his questions, to tell him to shut up. But he played the game. Teachers, in my experience, didn't do that kind of thing. They didn't banter with the class clown. They were always trying to get somewhere before the bell rang. They didn't have the confidence to risk being outsmarted by one of us.

Mr. Silver didn't seem to have anywhere to go. He didn't seem concerned with covering the chapter or even finishing the conversations we'd started.

"What's with the scribble, Mr. Silver?" Hala asked, exasperated by the conversation.

He smiled at her and turned back to Colin, "Are we finished?"

Colin nodded.

"Before we deal with the scribble let's deal with the, to be true to the *translated* text, paper knife. Hala, what does Sartre say about the paper knife?"

"He says that a letter opener," she smiled at him, flirting, "has an essence before it exists."

"Exactly. Unlike?"

"Unlike me."

"Meaning?"

"Meaning that according to Sartre we have no essence before we exist. Meaning that we, unlike a letter opener *or* a paper knife are here without some, like, preconceived plan for what we're here *for*."

Mr. Silver nodded his head slowly and smiled at Hala.

"Precisely," he said taking a dramatic pause. "And why is that relevant or interesting at all? Why should we care? What are the implications of that idea? What does it have to do with your lives? Why would Sartre have any reason to defend existentialism? After all, the purpose for giving this lecture in the first place was as a *defense* of existentialism."

Immediately, Colin answered. "Why should we take for granted that it even *is* interesting? That we *should* care? That there *are* any implications? That it has *anything* to do with our lives?"

Colin leaned back with his thin arms crossed across his chest and his eyebrows raised.

Mr. Silver looked at Colin. We were all watching him. He held Colin's gaze and then slowly a faint grin appeared.

"Would anyone like to answer Colin's questions?"

"Because, dude, one thing is that it totally denies the existence of God."

This was Lily who'd been sitting next to me drawing a looping design in her notebook. Lily, with her long hippie skirts and giant sweaters, her hemp bag and her ever-changing braids, looked down at her drawing and shook her head.

"What's your name?"

She told him, still looking down at her paper, her cheeks flushed as if embarrassed by her outburst and its passion.

"Go on, Lily," he said looking at Colin who was staring at the ceiling.

She took a breath and looked, for the first time, directly at Colin. She waited for him to make eye contact and when he did he shrugged his shoulders and widened his eyes aggressively.

"Look, man. If there's no plan for us before we're born then either God doesn't exist or he's just fucking with us. Sorry."

Silver shook his head, "Go on. Say what you have to say."

"O.K., so if God has no plan for us, or doesn't exist at all then a lot of people are going to be pissed off. So that's one thing. And the other thing is that if Sartre's right, if we're here and there's no reason then we're pretty much fucked. Sorry."

We laughed, thrilling at the novelty of obscenity in the classroom. Silver shrugged his shoulders, "Can anyone add to that? Is Lily right? Let's assume for the sake of this discussion that Sartre is right, that there is no plan and, even, that there's no God. Are we, as Lily suggests, 'pretty much fucked'?"

Sitting in the dead middle of the classroom, Abdul Al Mady, wide-eyed and nervous, nodded his head.

Silver turned to him. "This seems to interest you. Tell me your name."

"Abdul," he said quietly. "And, um, I, I don't know what you're saying really. God exists and it isn't right to say He doesn't. For sure there's a plan. It's written. I mean, it's written."

"Oh my God," Hala said to her desk.

"Go on," Silver encouraged him.

"Well, that's really it."

"The only person who's suggesting that God *doesn't* exist is Sartre. We're just using the possibility that he's right as a way to understand his philosophy."

"But He does exist."

"Oh my God." Hala again.

"Hala?" Silver raised his eyebrows.

"Abdul there *is* the possibility that he *doesn't* exist," she insisted.

Abdul repeatedly nodded his head, loudly blew the air out of his mouth and was otherwise silent.

"Abdul," Mr. Silver said, "I'm not suggesting that God does or does not exist. We're investigating someone else's ideas, trying to understand their ramifications, and so on. It's important to consider the views of other people don't you think?"

He said nothing. Hala looked like she might explode. Colin smirked. I studied Silver. Ariel played with her hair and rolled her eyes at Aldo. Aldo grinned and pushed his hair out of his eyes. Cara looked sympathetically at Abdul. Jane pretended to read Sartre. Lily moved her pen gracefully across her page as Rick squinted at Abdul.

"Look at the board. This, according to Sartre, is what we're born into. Remember, I'm not suggesting that he's right or wrong, only, Abdul, trying to explain his ideas. An orderless, meaningless life. We're born into this world with no specific purpose. No one said, 'Hmm, I know what I need for this job, I need a woman and boom a woman was made.' That's how a letter opener is born. It is not, according to Sartre, how human beings are born.

"For the record I will not preface each statement I make with 'according to Sartre.' You can all assume, unless I specifically tell you otherwise, I'm explaining his views and those of everyone else we'll discuss. Please don't go home and tell your parents that I'm a godless heathen who wants to convince you that your respective religions are absurd."

Everyone laughed except for Abdul, who sat there nodding over and over again. It was a strange way to disagree but it was his.

"So there's the problem: we're born and left to determine meaning, that is, '*L'homme est condamné à être libre.*' Anyone speak French?"

I raised my hand.

"Gilad. Will you translate for us please?"

"Man is condemned to be free."

"Good. And what do you think that means?"

I felt my heart beat faster and the blood rise to my face.

"Take a shot, Gilad."

"Choice is a curse."

"Bullshit." Colin again. Silver ignored him.

"Why would it be a curse?" he asked. I remember his eyes on me. I was embarrassed. I wanted to escape but I felt an intense desire to defend Mr. Silver.

"According to Sartre?" I asked.

"To begin with."

"I guess because if there's no God and we are free to make decisions then we're also responsible for those decisions."

He smiled at me with what I was sure was pride. He nodded.

"Beautifully said."

He looked at me for a moment and then went on, "So then, if there's no God and we're responsible for our decisions why would that be a condemnation?"

"Because everything we do is our fault," Rick said squinting up at the diagrams on the board.

"Why is it our fault? I don't really see that," Ariel said.

"Well, if God doesn't exist then it isn't *his* fault," Rick went on.

"But those aren't the only options. What about our parents, our environment, our families, where we're born, diseases, handicaps? Isn't it ridiculous to say that either it's God's fault or just our own?"

"That's not what he's saying," I said.

She turned to me.

"What?" She seemed amazed that I'd contradict her.

I thought how I wanted to touch her.

Silver sat on his desk with his arms folded watching us.

"What Rick just said . . . It's Rick, right?" I asked.

Rick had turned his attention from the board and was looking at me as he'd been looking at the diagrams.

"What Rick said, was that everything we *do* is our fault. Which seems to me exactly right. No matter what our parents do for a living, or where we grow up, or the diseases we have. We're still responsible for what we *do*."

"Whatever," Ariel said.

Silver pushed himself off his desk and looked coldly at Ariel.

"Tell me your name again," he said.

"It's Ariel, Mr. Silver." She seemed surprised that he didn't remember.

"Ariel, right. You may or may not agree with Gilad but 'whatever' is an inappropriate response. Gilad spoke clearly and respectfully. Your dismissal of his comments only reveals your own shortcomings. Don't do it again. Please."

There was a long pause. Ariel's pale face had turned red.

"If you have something intelligent to say please say it."

She pursed her lips and raised her eyebrows at Silver. "O.K., O.K.." She smiled at him. "I'm sorry, you're right."

Lily said, "So what's with the scribble?"

He laughed. "The scribble," he said, looking finally away from Ariel, "is what human lives are—disorganized, meaningless, purposeless, insignificant, and without order."

"Bummer," Lily said.

"Maybe," he said, and drew a grid over the chaos. "So what's this?"

I knew.

I watched him, praying he'd call on me until he did.

"It's what we pretend life is."

"Meaning?"

"Oh!" Hala said. "Like, religion is the grid."

"Go on."

Lily looked up from her drawing, "So, all the stuff we do—

eating with our forks in the left hand and our knives in the right. All that shit, that's the grid?"

He smiled. "What else?"

"College. Jobs. Laws. Grades," Rick said angrily to the grid.

"So, what? Those things don't exist?"

"No, they do. They do exist," Hala said. "It's just that they exist because we made them exist. I mean we built the laws so that we'd have this idea that everything makes sense. We love everything in order. That's the thing with religion, Abdul. Religion makes us feel like everything's all organized. Like everything makes sense. Like there's no other answer."

"There *is* no other answer," Abdul said to his notebook.

Then the bell rang and I wrote at the bottom of my first page, "Abdul says there is no other answer."

"Good class," Mr. Silver said leaning against his desk. "See you tomorrow. Come back angry."

When I looked up he smiled at me.

* * *

The rest of the day I barely spoke. During my other classes I wasn't asked to say anything other than my name.

I ate my lunch alone on the picnic bench beneath the pine tree.

Rick walked by and nodded.

When I passed Lily in the hall she smiled and said, "Hey dude."

On the bus I sat alone.

I was unsettled. Nervous. I was in love the way you are with an actor or a guy on stage with a guitar. It's instantaneous, a combination of jealousy and desire. Need. You want to change yourself entirely.

That day walking from the bus along the boulevard I wanted to possess him. Be him. Have him smile at me again. I wanted to be right. I wanted to go to war for him.

I would fight for him and against anyone who wouldn't. It wasn't complicated. In the beginning love never is.

MARIE

I thought about him all summer. The whole time we were at our house in Biarritz. I thought about him every single day. At first I was giddy but soon that ended and I just felt lonely and embarrassed. I kept replaying the night, cringing at the way I'd behaved. I spent my days at the beach lying in the sun, determined to be beautiful when I returned to school. My sister was at the house for a few weeks and I nearly told her what had happened. Ariel was in the US with her family. I didn't miss her.

Except for when my sister was there I spent most of my time alone. Sometimes I'd have lunch with my mother. But I tried to avoid it. She'd started cutting photographs out of Vogue and leaving them on my bed. I'd come back from the beach and there they'd be just lying there. No note or anything. Just those models looking up at me. I'd throw them away and the next day there'd be more. She never said anything about it and neither did I. But when that started I tried to avoid her completely.

To be honest I'd never thought much about sex or I mean that sex had never interested me. I'd never had any real desire. It was a part of my life in the sense that it was a constant subject at school and with Ariel but it had nothing to do with me physically. Ariel was always saying how horny she was. I never felt anything like that. I mean before Colin sex was an abstraction. And then afterward, for a long time afterward, I could barely feel my body. It was just vacant.

I'd never masturbated. Never had an orgasm. Never. Not until that summer when I began to think about him, in bed at night listening to the ocean. And then during the day with my fingers pressed into the hot sand, I'd imagine him kissing me. Lying on my towel, I mean right in the middle of the day, I'd imagine his hands on my body, and I'd feel a flush, a warmth spread up my thighs, hot between my legs, my nipples pulsing. I ached. All of me all the time.

* * *

Colin. Somehow we were together. I don't know. We were all drinking on the Champ de Mars. Colin was there and we were drunk and we ended up kissing on a bench somewhere and then we were together. That's it. That went on for a while and he was nice to me. I mean, he was O.K. He used to tell me what to wear to school and I'd do it. Jeans, tight T-shirts, that kind of thing. After a few months he started to get on my nerves. He was pushy and always wanted to have sex. I wasn't necessarily against having sex, but I didn't like the pressure and he wouldn't shut up about it. And I don't know if I was ready or not but he just pushed and pushed so one day we had sex in my bedroom when my parents were away.

It was horrible. I mean everything about him was hard. His lips, his body, his face, the way he touched me, everything about him. It was over fast and there was a small spot of blood on the towel I'd laid beneath us.

That was it.

He was O.K. for a while. He was nice to me usually and sometimes he was funny. Then one night after a school play, a musical, it was *Mame*, we got on the bus together. They were the late buses and ours wasn't very full. We sat at the very back and were hidden away behind the seats. There were maybe ten or fifteen other kids toward the front and we were pretty much alone in the back. He'd been pushing me to go down on him. He didn't shut up about it.

That night he starts talking about it again. Whispering to me in the dark and finally I said, Fine, I'll do it, O.K.? But he meant right there in the bus. And he pushes and pushes and pushes and finally I said I'd do it. He pulls down his jeans and he takes out his penis and he's hard. Then he starts to push my head down with his hand and I put a little bit into my mouth and I'm breathing through my nose like Ariel told me but I feel sick, like I'm going to choke, and now he's got my hair in his fists and he won't let go and he starts to push up with his hips. I begin to panic and breathe faster and faster through my nose and try to stop but he's got his hands on my head and he's forcing himself into my mouth. I'm afraid to make any noise. I feel like I'm going to choke to death, like I'm suffocating, like I'm going to die right there and still I can't make any noise. I'm shaking my head and digging my nails into his thigh and trying to get away, to get my mouth away, to tell him to stop but I can't, no matter what I do, he's too strong and I can't get away and I'm crying and I can't breathe.

I felt myself lightheaded as if I might pass out. I was shaking and then he comes and the minute I feel it in my mouth I sort of gag and then vomit a little bit of it into his lap and he makes this noise, this noise I'll never forget, of complete disgust and disapproval. And he lets go of me and I pull my head up and wipe my mouth and my face with the sleeve of my sweater. He says, What the fuck, Marie? And I don't look at him. I just sit there staring at the back of the seat. I'm crying and crying and my nose is running but I sit up straight the way my mom would have wanted and try not to breathe. I just concentrate on a single point and think of going home, of being in the shower.

He kept talking and shaking my shoulder, and saying, What's wrong, Marie? What's wrong? Why are you crying? As if he didn't fucking know. Anyway, I stopped hearing him. After a while I didn't hear a thing he said, and when the bus stopped on my corner, I got off and walked home. I don't know if he followed me.

I got home and locked the door and walked upstairs. I took off my clothes and got into the shower. I never talked to him again.

WILL

I was eating lunch at the picnic bench beneath the pine tree when Mazin sat down across from me. He'd grown over the summer and seemed so much older.

"Dude I miss your class. I hate English now. I'm going to die of boredom."

"Come on, Maz. It'll take some getting used to. Give it a chance."

"No, man. It doesn't mean anything. We don't talk about, I don't know, stuff. It's all this analyzing paragraphs and shit. I miss our talks."

"But here we are having one now."

"Yeah, on my free period. Lame."

"I'm flattered you'd waste your free period with me, Maz."

"Yeah, well don't get too excited. Anyway Silver, school's a waste of my time."

"Carrot?"

"No man, I don't want a carrot, I want to know why I shouldn't just move to LA and start a band."

"Who says you shouldn't?"

"Please. Everyone."

"You realize, right, that this is a tired conversation? You know everything I'm going to tell you. It's the height of boring."

"No I don't. You're the height of boring. What are you going to tell me?"

"You've heard it all before, Maz."

"Oh come on. Tell me. Please."

"There's nothing to tell you. You want to move to LA and start a band? Go. Otherwise, shut up and do your homework."

"That's it? That's your advice?"

"You were asking for advice?"

"Obviously."

"Look, Maz, I've said it a thousand times. You do what you feel is right. But it's *do* what you feel is right, not talk about doing. You understand?"

"So you're saying I should drop out of school?"

I laughed. "You know exactly what I'm saying."

"Yeah."

"Maybe moving to LA to become a rock star isn't the best alternative to doing your homework."

He got up and smiled at me. "I'm glad we can still have these talks, man. You never let me down. I got to go to class. I'll tell you if I decide to move to LA." He gave me a complicated handshake. The hugging had stopped.

"Peace, Mr. Silver."

* * *

That afternoon, I went with Mia to the Marché d'Aligre where we shopped for dinner. Afterward, we ate oysters and stayed late drinking too much wine at Le Baron Rouge and then went back to her apartment. I sat at the bar that separated her tiny kitchen from the living room and watched her cut small red potatoes into quarters.

I loved being there that evening—watching her cook, setting the table, following her orders, waiting for our guests. In the long cobbled courtyard below, a group of boys was playing soccer and with each goal came a burst of noise. I leaned out the window to watch the game.

Mia opened a bottle of wine and brought me a glass.

"Cheers," she said.

"Cheers."

"It's getting dark earlier and earlier."

I nodded.

"I say the same things every year," she said.

A boy in a green T-shirt scored a goal, raised his hands above his head, did a victory lap, and then disappeared into the building. Quickly the game dissipated and soon the court-yard was empty and quiet.

We didn't know Séb and Pauline very well, but Mia was always looking to befriend French people, who were, to her surprise and disappointment, difficult to know. So, after the four of us had drinks together a few weeks before, she called and invited them for dinner.

In those years, it felt that having dinner with other Americans was a kind of failure, that the purer, more authentic experience was always with the French and she was happy to have met Parisians she liked. She'd been taking cooking classes and had become a confident and talented cook. This would be her first dinner for a French couple and she was thrilled.

"You realize, Will, that this is one of the fantasies?"

"Which?"

"The Paris fantasies. To cook a French meal, for French people, in my Parisian apartment."

"Well, you'll do it beautifully."

"Thank you, William." She smiled at me.

"They're here," I said.

Séb and Pauline had pushed the heavy wooden door open, allowing a brief swell of street noise, before it closed behind them.

"*Salut,*" Mia called down.

They waved at us. We watched them holding hands, their footsteps echoing in the courtyard. Mia returned to the kitchen and I went to let them in.

The three of us drank wine and watched as Mia dredged pieces of sole through flour while butter melted in an iron skillet.

We ate at a small table in the living room. Mia insisted that we all sit before she would serve us and then one by one, she delivered plates of *sole meunière* and small bowls full of roasted potatoes. Séb, who worked for a wine distributor, opened one of the three bottles of *chablis grand crus* he'd brought.

"To new friends," Mia said and raised her glass. Her face was flushed from the kitchen heat, those wisps of hair falling around her face.

"To new friends," we all repeated and touched glasses.

After we'd eaten, after the requisite jokes were made about the rarity of Americans who could cook, and Parisians who could smile, after we talked about Chirac's noble defiance of George Bush, Mia asked how Séb and Pauline had met.

"It was the simplest thing," Pauline said. "We were in a café. Both of us alone at the bar having our coffee. Both of us reading our papers. Séb smiled at me. I smiled back. He said, *bonjour,* and that was it. We've been together since."

She touched the back of his neck and moved her fingers through his hair.

"*She* smiled at me," Séb said, "but everything else is true."

Pauline looked at Mia and rolled her eyes.

"How long has it been?" I asked.

"Nearly eight years," Pauline said. "I'd just finished law school."

"And you?" Sèb asked. "How did you two meet?"

"Oh, we're not—" Mia began.

"We're not together," I said.

They both laughed.

"You're serious?" Pauline looked amazed.

"Friends," I said.

"I don't believe you," Séb said.

"*Moi non plus.*" Pauline smiled.

"No, it's true." Mia looked up and when Pauline saw her eyes, she stopped laughing.

"We just assumed."

"Oh, you're not the first," I said.

Mia began to clear and Pauline followed. When they were in the kitchen talking, Séb put his arms on the table and leaned forward.

"*Mais pourquoi?*" He asked, like I was a lunatic.

"*C'est ma faute,*" I said. "*Je sais pas.*"

He looked at me for a long moment and then shook his head.

* * *

After they'd gone, I washed the dishes while Mia sat at the bar finishing the second bottle of wine. Then I felt her behind me. My hands were in the warm water. She wrapped her arms around my waist. She pulled me harder against her and kissed my neck.

"Mia."

She turned her head to the side and pressed it against my back. We stood like that, her arms around my waist, my hands in the water.

* * *

As I walked home, there was the familiar crush of isolation, that bodily loneliness that swept through me every winter. It was as if I'd been injected with something cold and viscous. I could feel it spreading through me, falling heavy in the center of my chest, pooling there. It was bitter and it was devastating and it frightened me.

* * *

From time to time I'd pass Marie in the hallway and she'd give me a knowing look. In those early days of the school year, passing her in the halls, I'd meet her eyes and feel a slight surge of desire. There was nothing more. I didn't think about her and wasn't much tempted. She pouted, flipped her hair and led with her breasts. She took on the manner-isms of an older, more confident woman, and none of it appealed to me.

* * *

The morning of October fourth I stood at the Odéon *métro* waiting for my train.

It was just before eight. People milled around, reading their papers, looking at their watches.

I'd been there maybe ten minutes already when a man my age arrived. The trains were slow that day.

"*Pardon,*" he said. "*Excusez-moi, ça fait longtemps que vous attendez?*"

Taller than me, he was wearing a suit, a black overcoat, a gray scarf wrapped twice around his neck. I was struck by him. Everything in place. Everything considered. It was a quality that I had, before moving to Paris, associated with elegant women. I admired these Parisian men, their precision, their attention to detail.

He was clean-shaven, wore thin-framed, rectangular glasses. His hair cut short, maybe half an inch long.

"*Dix minutes environ*," I said.

He thanked me, looked at his watch and blew air through his closed lips—a national gesture acknowledging that life is and will always be this way. Then there was the sound of the train.

"*Le voila.*"

"*Enfin,*" I said smiling.

The train came fast into the station. Just as it did I sensed a flash of movement behind me and to my left. And then in an instant the man shot forward. The rushing train slammed into his body with a dull muffled noise and he vanished.

Someone screamed. My eyes went clear, I stepped back immediately turning to my left, bracing myself, and saw a large, haggard man standing alone. We locked eyes, unblinking. I didn't move. He nodded at me as if I were somehow involved, turned and began to walk toward the exit. I watched him go and imagined tackling him to the ground.

I heard footsteps pounding behind me, coming from the other end of the platform. Someone ran past and drove his shoulder into the man's back. There was more screaming.

I did nothing.

Soon the station was filled with police.

I was sweating. And then I saw Gilad standing alone. He'd been waiting for the same train. He watched me come toward him. I stopped in front of him.

"You saw it?"

"Yes," he whispered.

"Come on," I said.

We walked to the Luxembourg Gardens and sat down on a bench beneath some trees. There was no one there. It was very cold. I was nauseated. I called the school and explained what had happened, that I wouldn't be there, that I'd need a sub, that Gilad was with me, that he wouldn't be at school, the *métro* wouldn't be running for a while.

I didn't know what to do next so the two of us sat there in silence in the cold park. I kept imagining the man with his white scarf, his delicate glasses and his immaculate clothes. Although I hadn't seen them, I thought about his fingernails. I was sure they'd been neatly manicured.

"*Ça fait longtemps que vous attendez?*"

"*Ça fait longtemps que vous attendez?*"

"*Ça fait longtemps que vous attendez?*"

"*Le voila.*"

I wondered about his glasses, whether they'd been broken. I watched him die over and over again. I listened to the sound of the train hitting his body. It was the sound of a heavy duffel bag hitting a concrete floor.

My phone rang several times but I didn't answer it. They wanted my lesson plans.

Eventually I stood. Gilad looked up with the same expression he'd had on the platform. As if asking, What happens now?

"We can go to a café I like."

We took a table in the mezzanine and ordered *cafés crèmes*. When they came we wrapped our hands around the warm cups.

"Did you see it?" I asked him.

"Yes."

"I mean you saw it happen?"

"Yes."

"You O.K.?" I asked him.

"Yeah. You know, I've seen bad things before. Violence. I don't know. The thing is I saw you first." He was playing with his spoon, turning it slowly through his coffee. "I saw you standing there. I recognized you and was thinking of maybe coming over to say hello or something. And then I saw that homeless guy, he was pacing around you know, and all of a sudden he just spun and charged and from where I was standing, it looked like it was you he was going to push. I mean it could have been you."

I nodded.

"Actually, I thought it was you, you know? I mean when that man went forward I saw you, not him. I mean I saw you being hit by the train."

This kid with his shaved head and his dark blue eyes. He bit his nails and looked from me to his coffee cup and back again. He was waiting for me to say something but I didn't know what to tell him.

I hadn't considered how close we'd been standing.

"It's really messed up, Mr. Silver. But I'm glad it wasn't you."

I smiled at him.

"I wish I had something important to tell you, something that might explain but I've got nothing."

"There is nothing."

"You don't think so?" I asked, looking at my hands, hearing the sound again and again.

Ça fait longtemps que vous attendez?

"No. I don't think so. I don't think so at all. I think it's just the way it is. I agree with Sartre."

"No God?"

"No God."

"Not very cheery."

"What, you believe in God, Mr. Silver?"

"I don't know."

That man in his fine coat crushed by the train.

"No," I said. "I'm with you. You and Sartre."

"I like your class, Mr. Silver. You know, I think maybe I've learned more in a month than I've ever learned anywhere."

"That's nice of you to say, Gilad. Thank you. You don't talk much. It's hard to tell."

"Yeah, well I like it. I think somehow your class has made

today make more sense. I understand better somehow. If you know what I mean."

"Really? No, I don't. I don't know. I don't understand it."

"I guess I've stopped thinking that the world should make any sense. It stops you from being disappointed. You know when you're always looking for some sort of logical explanation and stuff. I mean I haven't believed in God for a long time, but even still, up until this year I've always believed that there was some, I don't know, system, some kind of universal balance or something. Like, if I gave a certain amount I'd receive a certain amount. I guess, I don't know, I've always believed I'd be rewarded in the end just for being good. Or no, not really, not even for being good, just for, I don't know. Just for suffering."

He looked embarrassed by this last sentence and waved his hand as if to erase it. "I don't know, whatever."

I nodded. "For suffering?"

"No, no forget it."

"Tell me."

"I don't know, like the shit you go through. Whatever problems a person has. I guess I've always had this idea that if you endure it, you know? You handle yourself, take care of yourself, I don't know, like just get through it without becoming a total asshole you get rewarded in the end."

"By?"

"I don't know, by the universe?"

I nodded, "And you don't feel that way anymore?"

"No. It makes much more sense that you do what you can. I mean given what you've been given and then, then you just hope for the best. The whole idea that you deserve something, some kind of reward, I don't know, it's just. What am I? Ten? Come on, Mr. Silver."

I liked Gilad. He seemed such a lonely kid. He rarely smiled and when he did it was cynical and accompanied by a knowing nod usually in response to a comment he found idiotic.

My heart had slowed and the waves of nausea had subsided, leaving me weak and cold. The sun shone through the front window of the café and the room became bright. I squinted and turned my head away. It was nearly noon. The two of us had been sitting there together for a long time, neither of us speaking.

I took a breath. Again I felt like I needed to tell him something. But as miserable as he looked I had nothing to offer.

* * *

That night I stayed late at La Palette and sat in the back corner near the window facing the open room. It wasn't crowded, only a few couples and a group of girls laughing and drinking champagne. I ordered beer after beer from the white-bearded waiter who always called me *mon vieux* and shook my hand when I walked through the door. Eventually the girls stood up and left, taking with them whatever hope was left in the night.

I sat and waited for something to happen. And then, incredibly, wonderfully, it did. My phone vibrated with a message from Marie. *I'm close. Do I come over?*

I waited pretending to contemplate the decision. And when it felt as if enough time had passed, I answered, paid the check, said good-bye, and walked home.

She came up the stairs and into the apartment. Long dark hair. Too much make-up. A tight black T-shirt. Short, pale-green skirt. She balanced awkwardly on a pair of high heels.

"Sit down."

She drew out the chair and sat in it, placing her purse on the table.

"Does anyone know you're here, Marie? Honestly."

"No one." She raised her eyes and met my gaze with a determined stare, a slight grin on her face.

I nodded. She smelled like cigarettes and alcohol. Something sweet. Her lips shone. I imagined her standing in the stairwell, carefully applying gloss. I looked at her but said nothing.

"Aren't you cold?" She wrapped her arms around herself and shivered. She looked across the room at the open window. "Oh you can see the Eiffel Tower," she said, standing and walking toward it.

I turned in my chair. She walked back slowly, looking around the room. "I love your place."

"So why'd you come?"

"Why'd you tell me to come?"

"I was curious. Why'd you come?" I asked again.

She was nervous and walked to the long kitchen counter, leaned against it, her back to me.

Having her there calmed me. I felt suddenly in control. I could breathe.

"Do you like this, Marie?"

"Like what?" She asked turning from the counter.

"Showing me your body like you are, letting me watch you."

She smiled. "You like my body?"

"I do."

"What do you like?"

I looked at her facing me—arms spread out behind her, fingers on the countertop, her breasts full. I was absorbed by her body, all of it offered so certainly. And though I knew she was playing at seduction, I created her for myself, made her what I wanted.

"I'll tell you precisely. Would you like that?"

She hopped up onto the counter, dangling her legs. "Yes," she said.

I waited, studied her face, searched for some indication of fear. But there was only determination.

"I like the curve of your breasts, I like your ass, the way you move, as if wherever you're going is the most important place you'll ever go. I like your hair. I like your lips, how they're full the way your breasts are. That's what I like. Of what I've seen, anyway," I said.

Her face had flushed, her cheeks made redder in the low light cast by the lamp on the dresser. She looked, before she raised her chin to speak, like a girl receiving praise from a proud parent. There were those wide pleading eyes and her face turned to me. I did my best to suppress my instinct to change course. But I felt the weight return softly to my chest, my heart began to pound and the clarity I'd felt minutes before was lost.

"I—" she said.

"Wait," I told her, and walked into the bathroom. I closed the door. I stood above the toilet and took out my cock, which minutes before had begun to harden and was now flaccid in my hand. I pissed into the water and closed my eyes.

Finished, I stood in front of the sink and ducked the mirror.

I wet my hands with cold water and ran them over the back of my neck.

She was still sitting on the counter leaning slightly forward so that her hair fell across her face. I leaned against the open bathroom door.

"Do you know why I came here?"

I shook my head. She hopped from the counter and I felt the night slow and slow and slow until it looked as if Marie were flying, her arms propelling her outwards, her swinging legs bringing her toward me. I saw her hands leave the counter, her body arch through the air. She landed and I could breathe again. She looked me dead in the eyes and said, "You know why I came here, Mr. Silver? I came here to fuck you."

I laughed but she didn't flinch.

"I did," she said. "That's why I came here." I smelled cigarettes and that sweetness like overripe apples. I raised my hand and slid my fingers into her hair. At the base of her skull it was soft, but as I moved outwards there was the hardness of hairspray. I took a step closer so that my lips were inches from hers. She was breathing quickly, her eyes shone with a steady determination, as if she were playing a character she couldn't quite inhabit.

And we looked at each other, the two of us in a room, in a building, in a city in the world. I was far enough away to see us there. I took a deep breath and then her knee was between my legs, her arms around my neck.

She held on tightly, desperately, moaning as if she were in pain. She turned her back. She moved up and down, stroking me, my hands cupping her breasts, my mouth at her neck. I wrapped my arms around her, holding her with strength until she slowed slightly.

She spun and faced me again, bit my lip, ran her hand over the fly of my jeans, felt how hard I was and smiled at me, victorious. I grasped her hair tighter, pulled her head back and kissed her neck softly. She squeezed my cock tight. I pushed my hand up her skirt, slid her panties away, and felt her slick. I stroked her gently, gliding my forefinger lightly between her lips. She moaned but now guttural. She squeezed me too hard. I pulled her hand away. She opened her eyes and looked at me, frightened.

"Gentle," I whispered, and pushed my two middle fingers deep into her cunt. She exhaled fast and made the same, rough moan. "Oh my God," she said quietly. "Fuck."

I pushed deeper and pressed my palm against her clit. I held her like that, barely moving. "I can't stand anymore," she said. "I want to go up."

"Take off your clothes," I said.

She stood in front of me, pulled her t-shirt over her head, reached behind her and unfastened the clasp of her bra.

"You're beautiful," I told her.

"Take off your clothes," she told me.

I pulled my shirt over my head as she unzipped her skirt. She stood in her panties, looking at me. I paused. "Go on," she said, smiling. "Shy?"

I unbuttoned my jeans and stepped out of them. She looked at my body. "All."

I slid my underwear down and stood in front of her naked. "You."

She left hers on the floor. I walked to her.

"Up," I whispered, moving her toward the ladder to my bed. I stayed close to her as we climbed, as she stepped tentatively upwards. I'd left the window open and the air was cold. We slid into bed together with her back to me. I wrapped my arms around her warm body, she sighed a long slow sigh. In that moment I felt the tremendous physical relief of finding someone there with me, the sense that something missing had been returned.

I kept her close to me, smelling her hair, stroking her skin. She gave in completely. Softened. And for a while we were still. There was street-noise outside, bursts of laughter, glasses breaking in the café below. I felt her back expanding against my chest. We were still until she reached between my legs and fitted the head of my cock inside her. I moved slow until I was deep, until I could feel her so warm, impossibly soft, so tight around me.

"Oh my God," she said. *"Oui, c'est bien ça."*

Outside there was more noise. A crash. Crying. Breaking glass. Silence. Then laughter in the café again.

"What was that?" she whispered.

"Friday night. Who knows? Marie, I'm going to put on a condom."

"Yes, Jesus, I forgot. Hurry up."

I slid into her gently. Now she was on her back and kept a hand on her belly and as I slid deeper she said, "Gentle."

I began to move. She clawed at me. When I stopped she told me not to. "Please," she said, "don't stop, please," and pulled me down so that my chest was against hers.

She said, "I want to hear you come."

"So soon? What about you?"

"I've never," she told me.

"Please," she said. "Come loud."

As I moved faster and faster she dug her nails hard into my skin. She bit my shoulder. She moaned her strange low moan, louder and louder. "Please," she said again and again, "come for me." When I cried out she said, "Yes, yes," and caressed the back of my head, so slow.

That tenderness surprised me. I was grateful for it. Then I wished the whole thing hadn't happened. And I knew it would again.

* * *

I was standing at the top of my stairwell shirtless in a pair of jeans when she kissed me good-bye. Then she was the brave girl. Tough with her purse, and a new coat of lip-gloss.

"Goodnight," I said.

"Goodnight," she smiled, and shook her head. "This is crazy. O.K., I have to go. Bye, Mr. Silver. I'm leaving now."

She closed the door and I stood in the center of the room, in the dark, in the blowing wind, listening to her footsteps fading as she descended the stairs, and when I couldn't hear her any longer I walked to the open window.

There were a few people left sitting at tables in the yellow light of Bar du Marché. Marie came out onto the street, passed in front of the café and walked fast toward boulevard St. Germain.

It was nearly dawn and she was alone. I could hear her shoes clicking against the pavement. I wondered where she was going and how she'd get there. I hadn't asked and as I saw her vanish around a dark corner, I felt a quick sense of dread.

MARIE

I'd spent the entire summer lying in the sun thinking about him. I barely ate. I was so tan. Everyone told me I looked great. When my dad showed up for a few days he kissed me on the forehead and told me I was beautiful.

Even my mother. The first day of school I'd come down wearing a loose black embroidered top she'd bought for me from Isabel Marant. And I had the bag she'd given me too, not a backpack, but a woman's bag, a pretty leather Jerome Dreyfuss sac which was totally unrealistic and just like her.

I came down the stairs and she turned around. *Oh Marie*, she said. She had her hands at her face. She was beaming. *Oh Marie, qu'est ce que t'es belle, ma chérie! Mon dieu, qu'est ce que t'es belle.* I thought she was going to cry. And maybe she did a little bit. She came over and kissed me. *Oh la la, Marie. Oh la la. T'es belle.* I was so happy that morning. We sat together and ate our *tartines* with coffee and it felt as if everything would change, like we were celebrating together the rest of my perfect life. Now I was beautiful. And at school, waiting for me, was this man, this man, this tender man.

* * *

Over the summer I began to masturbate. Not just nervous experiments. I'd take a bath then lock the door to my bedroom. I'd get into bed and with the lights off and the windows open, listening to the ocean at the bottom of the cliffs, I'd close my eyes and think about him kissing me. I felt completely in myself. As if in those evenings there was no separation between my self and my body. I was just there. It was as if I were drunk. Soon I learned to make myself come. There was no going back. All summer was like a love affair.

So walking downstairs that morning, seeing my mother look at me like that, I mean for the first time in my memory just completely satisfied, and sitting with her eating breakfast together and knowing that I'd see him. Oh, it was like everything was laid out in front me. As if finally, finally, I don't know, something had changed.

It was pathetic. What was my plan exactly? But at the time, it all made so much sense.

* * *

At school it was as if I didn't exist. I did everything I could to run into him, to pass him while he was eating lunch or in the hall when I knew he was on his way to class. Of course he wanted nothing to do with me. He wasn't rude or even cold. He just treated me like anyone else, like any other student. He'd smile, maybe hold my gaze a few seconds longer than was safe, but that was it. It ruined me. I was so surprised. Then I was angry at myself for being surprised. How could I have been so stupid and all that. But those first few weeks, the first month, all of September I was thrown, and everything seemed to get worse and worse.

I'd planned to cut myself off from Ariel, to pull away from her, just kind of drift. Nothing dramatic. I'd be strong and passive. But when I realized that he wasn't going to do anything at all, that he wouldn't take a step, I went back to my old life. It felt like such a defeat but there I was at Ariel's apartment on Friday nights. She pretended to feel sorry for me but it was clear that she was thrilled. What's worse is that she was in his class and got to see him every day. She'd tell me what a great teacher he was, how he was always staring at her. Once she said, If I get him I promise we'll share him Marie, we'll have a little threesome. I thought I was going to punch her.

One Sunday at her apartment we got up and her parents were both there. They'd come back from some trip and were in the kitchen making scrambled eggs and toast. We ate together and I remember having a good time. It was nice. You know, pass the salt and all that. It was strange in their giant apartment, usually so quiet and still, and then that morning really filling the kitchen. All of us talking. Ariel was so happy, just sort of bouncing around, really at ease and without any of her usual stiffness. She laughed a lot and I remember thinking it was the first time I'd ever heard her laugh naturally.

Anyway, it was nice. Her parents were warm. I mean in the way that people like that are warm. It was as if they were our guests and we were people they really liked and they were happy to be there but you always knew that they would leave at the end of the party.

Her father was a big guy. Tall and wide with red hair. He was loud and had these huge hands. I think he'd been some kind of athlete. I liked him. He was just who he was. There was no formality at all. He looked at you when he spoke. Everything was simple with him. No subtext. Ariel's mother was O.K. too. She was pretty of course. So much smaller than her husband and thin like Ariel. She looked at me the way Ariel did. Assessing. Just like my mother.

After breakfast Ariel and I went to study in her room. At some point she left to go running and I stayed on her bed with my books open in front of me. I must have been working on a paper for Ms. Keller. I worked hard for her. She was the only one of my teachers I cared about and who seemed to care about me. I was trying to figure out some poem and all of a sudden he was there drinking a cup of coffee, standing in the doorway smiling at me. He asked what I was working on. I told him and he came in. It didn't feel strange to have him there. I mean, I didn't feel uncomfortable or threatened. He told me how he never liked poetry or something like that. I was lying on my stomach facing away from the door and he sat down next to me. He sipped his coffee and looked at the page trying to figure the thing out. And then he said something like, I don't know Marie, this might be over my head. Then he laughed his big wide-open laugh and put his hand on my shoulder. But he was just patting me you know? Like, O.K. I'll let you get back to work. Hang in there. That kind of thing. Then Ariel came back and we both turned around. She was standing at the door in her running clothes looking at us.

Know anything about poetry, Ariel? he said. She didn't say anything, or not that I remember anyway. She looked pale. She shrugged her shoulders and went to take a shower. She barely spoke to me the rest of the day.

* * *

Ariel never said a thing about it, but you could tell she hated me. It was over, you know? A week later we went out to this bar in the fifth, The Long Hop. Aldo was there, Mazin, and some other people I don't remember. We were all drunk. The place was crowded and there were maybe, I don't know, five of us at this little table. And then Colin shows up and sits down on some girl's lap and smiles at me. I ignored him.

I mean he'd been around. It's not like it was the first time

I'd seen him since. But God his face made me sick. Seeing him there that night, I wish I could say that I only felt anger but the truth is that when he sat down I was afraid too. It's a blur but at some point Ariel says, How's Mr. Silver? And I think she's talking to Colin because they're both in his class but then I see she's looking at me. And everyone's looking at Ariel waiting for the point. So she asks again and I say, I don't know. She says, Oh come on, Marie tell them. I look at her horrified and she says, Fine I'll tell them.

Marie hooked up with Mr. Silver. After that I don't remember what happened exactly. Just that Colin said it was bullshit. In your dreams, he said. Then I didn't know who I hated more. My face was so hot and everyone was staring at me. They must have seen it. I turned to Ariel and I called her a bitch and I left.

I went to the river and walked fast and then I stood out on that bridge, it was the Petit Pont I think, or the Pont au Double and I stood there not knowing what to do feeling completely alone. Like it had never quite occurred to me before, the idea that I was really alone. Or that's how it felt. And there I was in my stupid skirt, in that fucking outfit Ariel had chosen for me, and I was shivering and I just thought fuck it and I sent him a message. I wrote, "I'm in your neighborhood should I come?"

I waited looking down into the river watching the boats go by. Then, like a miracle, he said yes.

I walked along the river on the *quai* side past all the locked up *bouquinistes*. It wasn't until I reached the Pont Neuf that I really thought about what I was doing, where I was going. I'd been walking in a fury thinking about Ariel. She knew what had happened with Colin. She'd promised to hate him. She'd wanted to call the police. Tell her parents or something. And there she was sitting in that bar with him laughing at me. It's all I could think about, but when I reached the Pont Neuf and I crossed the street to walk up the rue Dauphine I realized where

I was going. It slowed me down. I took my time walking up that street but I didn't once think I wasn't going to do it.

He lived on the top floor. No elevator and this little uneven stairwell that went around and around, up and up. At the top the door was open. When I walked in he didn't do anything but look at me. I was a mess. My heart was beating so hard. The minute I saw him, all I wanted was for him to wrap his arms around me. Just walk over and take me in your arms. But he didn't and I didn't know what to do with myself.

Somehow I ended up sitting on his kitchen counter. I don't remember. I just tried to be tough. I told him I came there to fuck him. I mean if you can imagine. I came here to fuck you, Mr. Silver, I said. He must have thought I was a joke. He watched me with those eyes and that smile like he was so fucking smart. Like he pitied me a little bit. As if he saw everything, knew everything about me. The prick.

At some point he touched me. He came forward and slid his hands into my hair and then it was over. I mean never in my life have I felt so out of control as I did with him. It isn't as if he was some big super-masculine guy who just wrapped me up and took me away. But there was something about him I swear to God. I could feel the warmth of his hand against my neck, you know, his fingers touching my skin and all I felt, I swear, was thank God, thank God, thank God you're touching me. I was so grateful. With my whole body I was grateful and relieved. And then he kissed me the way he kissed with that soft slow fucking tender gentle you're the love of my life way so that I could barely stand.

I took off my clothes. He made me do it for him while he watched. I was so cold and the window was open and the apartment was cold too, and it was as if I'd been shivering for hours. But I did it and he smiled at me and there was something in that smile that reminded me of the way my mother looked at me when I came down the stairs the first day of school. Then it became a game. I mean I relaxed and I pushed back a little bit, I told him to take off his own fucking clothes and he liked that I think. We laughed together and Christ what a relief that was, the two of us laughing, and then I was so glad to be there. Then all I wanted was him to take me up to his bed. There was nowhere else I wanted to go. Nowhere else.

I watched him. He never looked away from me. Not even to step out of his jeans. He was in O.K. shape. I mean he was stronger than I'd imagined. He had hair on his chest and on his legs. It frightened me. Not that I found it unattractive. Or attractive. Or anything really at all. Just that I noticed it. Then he pulled off his underwear. I was embarrassed as if it was too much for me to see even if I *did* see. I mean it was the first time I'd seen a man standing naked like that. I turned away and started climbing up. I noticed he'd made his bed and I thought that was nice, that the sheets were clean and the pillows were in their place. Then I got under the comforter and it was maybe the most wonderful thing I'd ever experienced in my life up to that moment. I mean I was so cold and then there was this man there, and I was sliding into his bed, slipping in like that with the sheets cool against my skin.

Then he was there behind me, his arms, his body. He was hard against me. He held me so tight. He was very warm and smelled good like lemons and ocean water and I closed my eyes and just waited there. I could feel the hair on his chest pressed against my back. Then there was his mouth against my neck. He wasn't really kissing me, just sort of holding his lips against my neck and I could feel him breathing, could hear him sort of sigh and I thought, maybe this matters to him. Maybe he feels something.

The way he touched me, I mean everything he did was strong you know? He seemed so certain of himself. Or maybe it was just that he was practiced. I don't know. It felt good. I was afraid for a lot of it. Afraid of him. I felt out of control. I mean I would have let him do anything he wanted to me. Anything. He was so slow the way he put it inside me like that, just a millimeter at a time, that I felt like I was losing myself. I didn't even think about the condom. It didn't even occur to me. He was the one who said it. I'm going to put a condom on, Marie. But at that moment? I didn't care. Do what you want, I thought. Do whatever you want.

I had this sensation of falling, or maybe flying, of being in motion, of being in motion and somewhere else, away. And then all I wanted was for him to come, as if his coming would confirm something. When he did, when I felt him give in, he lay down next to me, and he was sweet. He kissed me and took me into his arms and we lay there together for a long time listening to the night outside with him stroking my back, my head on his chest.

I had to leave. I'd have never asked to sleep there, though that's what I wanted more than anything. I wanted to stay there and never leave the way you want things like that. But I got up and dressed and left him there. I left without having any idea where I was going. I didn't even think about it until I got into a cab and realized I'd have to go back to Ariel's. There was nowhere else to go.

She was asleep when I got there. I took off my clothes and got into bed with her and lay on my back looking at the ceiling feeling happy, so happy that I laughed out loud. I mean just a little laugh but it woke Ariel up.

I'm sorry, she said. I told her it was O.K. and she asked me where I'd been. I rolled over onto my side and looked at her. I mean I looked at her right in the face, right in the eyes, and told her everything.

GILAD

He was standing there with that leather bag slung over his shoulder. I'd see him walking into school returning a book or a magazine to its place, watch him buckling the straps. He didn't miss a thing that guy, paid attention to every detail, always played the part. I never saw him with anything ugly. He never would have shown up at school with a nylon backpack or an old computer case the way other teachers did.

That morning I saw the bag and I knew it was him. I was trying to figure out what I might say if I walked over. It's a long train ride and I couldn't imagine sitting with him all that time.

I didn't have the courage. When the train came ripping up the tracks I was disappointed. I was facing the train as it came and I saw the guy who'd been wandering around talking to himself charge toward Silver. I said, "No." I said it aloud, my eyes wide, everything slowing down. I saw the man bend where he was hit, square in the lower back so that his body looked like a loaded bow. He was so unprepared for it. His arms flew upwards, his head snapped back and then he went forward. There was a heavy thump and very fast he disappeared beneath the train.

I was sure it had been Silver. When I saw him still standing there I felt, at first, a brief surge of joy—because it hadn't been him, yes, but mostly because this thing that had happened would mean we now had to talk. It would be something between us, something shared.

He took me to a café across from the Luxembourg Gardens. Au Petit Suisse. We sat together at a table and drank coffee. I pretended to be more moved by what'd happened than I was. It was thrilling to be there with him, just two friends having coffee. I couldn't think about the man who'd died without being grateful for being there. I knew that I should have felt something. Sadness or shock. I played at it a little and the act made me feel comfortable in the long silences. I stared at the table and tried to think of something important and interesting, something impressive to say to Mr. Silver. He took this as sadness and tried to comfort me.

Not that I wasn't scared by what had happened. The violence had been sickening. The speed of it, the randomness, all of it scared me. But I was grateful to have been there, for that bond with him. I wouldn't have traded it. Not even for the guy's life. It was ours, exceptional, incredible, terrifying, and it connected me to him in a way none of his other students could be. I wouldn't have given that up. Never.

I remember wondering why he hadn't moved, why he'd done nothing, why he'd stood there staring, frozen in place.

* * *

When I returned home that afternoon my mom stood up from the couch and wrapped her arms around me. She'd been crying.

"The school called. They said you never showed up today. Jesus Christ, honey."

We sat on the couch. I told her about the train and about him. She listened and cried, holding my hand while I spoke. The leaves had turned but still it was warm enough to keep the windows open.

"It could have been you."

"Mom, I'm fine. He wasn't near me."

"Still. I'm so sorry you had to see that. Oh sweetie," she said squeezing my hands with hers. "I'll send a note to Mr. Silver. It was nice of him. You like him, don't you?"

"He's the best teacher I've ever had."

She smiled at me and touched my face. "I'm glad. That's lucky."

"Does Dad know?"

"No, not yet. He'll be home later. You can tell him then."

I shrugged.

She looked at me for a moment longer, "You know, honey, what you saw . . . "

"Mom, it's O.K., I'm not ruined, it's just something that happened."

She took my hand. "I'm not talking about today. I mean July."

I looked at her, anger rising.

"Listen, you *know* me, I'm not a victim, and I'm not one of those women who sits cowering in the corner."

I withdrew my hand.

"Gilad, you know very well that I'm not."

"I don't."

"You *do* know that."

"And yet you're still here."

"I should have left?"

I stood and looked down at her.

"You should've left," I said. "You should leave now. *We* should leave now."

WILL

I slept fitfully, finally gave up and got out of bed at five. The sky was that dark morning blue. The moon was up, some fading stars.

There were very few people on the streets. I stopped at Carton to buy a *pain aux raisins* from the humorless woman who pretended not to know me. I walked up rue de l'Ancienne Comédie past the unconscious homeless men on the grate, crossed Boulevard St. Germain, bought a copy of *Libération* and descended into the station. I stood alone on the platform. Across the tracks a man slept on the floor with his back turned toward me. There was a bottle on its side, wine in a black pool by his knees.

When I heard the train deep in the tunnel I turned and watched it come sweeping fast out of the dark. It arced toward me and blew into the station. As it passed I felt a chill of vertigo as if I were standing atop a very tall building looking down on the streets below. The car was empty. I took out a photocopied packet I'd put together for seminar and tried to read.

When I arrived at school the English department was locked. First in, I left the fluorescent lights off, turned on the lamp at my desk and made a pot of coffee. Outside the sky was turning pink. There was frost on the field. I sat at my desk with the paper and a cup of coffee and ate my breakfast.

The United States was preparing to invade Iraq. There had been protests throughout Europe and an enormous *manifestation* was planned for the coming weekend.

Toward the end of the paper was a short article about what had happened at Odéon the day before. A homeless man had shoved thirty-two-year-old Christophe Jolivet, a marketing executive from Nantes, in front of a train. Dead by the time emergency workers arrived. I took a pair of scissors from the ceramic cup on my desk and carefully cut out the article.

The fifteen-minute bell rang. I collected my things and walked down the hall to my classroom. Inside, the morning light was beginning to fill the room. I wrote the day's quotation on the clean white board and then I waited for the bell to ring.

* * *

They were all there except for Gilad.

"Has everyone read the packet?"

They nodded except for Colin who smirked at me. I raised my eyebrows.

"I didn't have time, sir."

"You didn't have time?"

"No."

"So why'd you show up today?"

"What do you mean?"

"Why are you here? In class today. Why'd you come?"

"It's not like I have a choice, sir."

I laughed. "We've covered this, haven't we?"

"Just because *you* say I have a choice doesn't mean I do."

"Ah, I see. I'll tell you what, challenge the idea. Why don't you get up and leave?"

"Because, sir, if I get up and leave, you'll report that to Mr. Goring and I'll end up in detention for skipping class."

"I won't tell anyone."

"How do I know I can trust you?"

"You have to make a choice Colin—you have to make a choice to trust me, in the same way you have to make a choice about staying in this class. I know you'd rather believe you're the subject of great oppression but the fact remains that you have a choice. Despite the powerful forces you seem convinced are keeping you down, you still have a choice. That may not be the case for Abdul but it is certainly the case for you."

Upon hearing his name, Abdul glanced up from his desk.

"Why would it be different for Abdul?" Ariel asked.

"Because, Ariel, Abdul believes in God."

"*And*?"

"And Colin doesn't."

"*And*?"

"And, *Ariel*," Rick said, shaking his head, "someone who believes in God might believe that *God* makes all their choices for them. They might believe that they're not responsible for their actions, that it's God who's responsible. But if you don't believe in God then who the hell *else* would be responsible for the choices we make?"

"Excuse me, Rick, but, I believe in God but I don't believe he makes my choices for me."

"And that's why I said might."

Abdul raised his hand.

"You don't have to raise your hand, Abdul," I said.

"Ummm, I just believe in God's plan. God has a plan for all of us and we just, you know, live that plan."

"So you're not responsible for anything you do? You're just a little puppet and God's pulling your strings? I mean, like what you just said? God made you say that?" Hala said looking at him in disbelief.

"Pretty much, yeah," Abdul said looking down at his desk.

"Are you kidding?"

"No," he whispered.

"God," Hala said in disgust. "You give us such a bad name."

He turned to her, "What do you *mean*?"

"Arabs. You make Arabs look like lunatics. You make us all look crazed with, like, Korans and bombs and, *God*, I mean wake up!"

Abdul's eyes were wide.

"O.K., that's enough. Hala, surely you'll grant Abdul the right to believe anything he wants to believe, right?"

"I guess. Maybe."

"Good. All of this began with Colin, so let's end it there. I'm giving you the choice, Colin. You can leave or you can stay. If you stop coming to class it will influence your class participation grade. However, I will not report your absences to the administration. A student shouldn't come to class if he or she doesn't want to. Frankly, arriving here without having read the material your class participation grade suffers anyway. You may as well leave. You seem to be sure you have better things to do. As I've said several times already, it's your choice."

Everyone stared at Colin. He stared at me. After a few moments he stood, took his backpack from the floor and left the room.

Lily let out a loud breath. "Oh my God."

The door closed quietly behind him.

It was the first time a student had ever called my bluff.

Abdul shifted in his seat. Ariel's expression suggested genuine surprise. Rick studied me. Jane smiled her shy smile. Aldo looked at Ariel for a cue. Cara tried to contain a rising laugh. Lily shook her head and said, "Dude," in disbelief. Hala watched me and chewed on her pen.

I took the photocopies from my desk and began handing them out.

"Each of you has the same right," I said. "I offer you all the same deal. If you feel that this class is somehow being imposed upon you, please don't come. My feelings won't be hurt. There are enough of you here who are interested in what we're doing, who have demonstrated real enthusiasm for the material. Those of you who feel that your time would be better spent doing something else, go do it."

When I'd finished handing out the article I sat on the edge of my desk and looked directly at Ariel.

"You're all free to do as you like."

She smiled at me as if I'd invited her for a drink.

I looked away. "Well, that's what I believe. What you have in front of you is an article from today's *Libération*. Hala, will you translate?"

"Sure." She took a breath and read the headline, "Man Killed: Pushed onto the Tracks of the *métro*." She looked up at me.

"Go on."

"Thirty-two-year-old Christophe Jolivet died Monday morning at the Odéon *métro* station after he was pushed in front of an arriving train. The attacker, twenty-nine years old, was psychologically . . . I don't know, I guess it would be, unstable. He's being held at the Sainte-Anne psychiatric hospital. He didn't seem to know the victim. The police say that he wasn't under the influence of drugs or alcohol but that he was in an excited state when he was arrested. According to the Police, he'd acted on a 'sudden impulse.' The attacker had a long history of violence. He was stopped and held by several morning commuters. Anne-Marie Idrac, speaking for the RATP, complimented the commuters for their courage and their composure. That's it. More or less."

"Thanks, Hala. Does anyone know why I've given this to you?"

"Because it sort of proves the point."

"What do you mean Cara?"

She was looking down at her desk making a wide circle with her finger around the article.

"It's just another example of how random the world is, how

nothing makes sense, how you can't make sense of anything. Everything's just, I don't know, a mess."

"How do you get that from this one story?" Ariel asked. "I mean, maybe the guy deserved it, maybe he was a horrible guy. I don't know maybe he was a drug addict or something."

Jane, who had barely spoken since the beginning of the year, jerked her head up and glared at Ariel, "That's just, that's, I'm sorry, but that's just the stupidest idea I've ever heard. You can't be serious."

"Excuse me?" Ariel snapped.

"Jane, perhaps there's a better way to disagree? Try to explain yourself."

"Sorry," she said to the desk, tapping her finger on her notebook.

"Go on, Jane."

"Well, I just, I don't know. It's hard to explain."

"Try anyway," I said.

She sat there looking at the whiteboard behind me. Her round face was bright red and a rash was descending from her chin down her neck. She took a long breath, "I just think the idea that this guy somehow deserved to die like that because he might have been a . . . a . . . what? What did you say? A drug addict? That's just, it's just like something, it just makes no sense to me. I just don't believe that everything that happens can be, I don't know. Like you can explain it."

"But wasn't that the point of what you read for class? That *you* can't explain it but God has his reasons and that we must simply trust in God?" I asked.

"I'm sorry but that's just . . . "

"Bullshit, man." This was Lily.

Aldo laughed and Lily turned to him, "Dude, do you *ever* say anything intelligent or do you just grunt and follow Ariel around like a puppy?"

"O.K., O.K., O.K.. Enough. Everyone calm down."

The door opened and Gilad walked in. He handed me a note. I read it, gestured for him to sit down and gave him a copy of the article.

"We were just discussing this."

He glanced at the headline and looked up at me and nodded. "I saw it."

Abdul raised his hand.

"You don't need to raise your hand, Abdul."

"O.K., the thing I wanted to say is that we don't, it's that, I agree. I agree with her."

He said this looking at his hands.

"With whom?"

"With her," he said shooting a glance over at Ariel who was glaring at him.

"O.K.," I said. "Go on."

"Well, God does everything for a reason. Everything that happens on earth happens because, because God has a plan."

Ariel, obviously sharing none of Abdul's conviction, looked out the window. Hala dramatically dropped her head into her hands. And Gilad, quiet Gilad, turned to Abdul and asked very simply, "What?"

Abdul looked so meek and frightened. It took such energy for him to make his proclamations, yet he couldn't seem to help himself, as if he were afraid he'd be punished for being silent.

"Yeah," he said, nearly whispering. "Everything happens for a reason. It's, just, it's, um, it's what I said. God's plan." He scratched the back of his hand.

"I was there." Gilad looked up at me. "We were both there. Yesterday, we were on that platform. I was there with Mr. Silver. We saw the guy get pushed. I watched him die. I *watched* him get smashed by that train. I *saw* that man push him. I saw it. And you're saying that *God* was punishing him for, for what? For something he'd *done*? That there was some reason? That

God has a plan? That *this* was part of his plan? Abdul, it could have been Mr. Silver. Do you understand that?"

Abdul looked at the ceiling and took a deep breath, "Yes. It wasn't. You saw it. It was part of his plan."

Gilad shook his head.

"Dude, Mr. Silver," Lily said, "you guys *saw* that yesterday? That's fucked *up*. Sorry."

Aldo snorted, caught Lily's glare, and went immediately silent.

"Yes, that's why Gilad and I weren't in school yesterday. And that's why, in part, I brought in the article. Everything we've discussed so far, even the question of choice, is relevant to the text you read over the weekend. If you'll take a look at the board, you'll see God's first question to Job and his subsequent command, 'Where wast thou when I laid the foundations of the earth? Declare, if thou hast understanding.' Everything that's happened to Job—God's seemingly cruel and random acts—simply can't be understood by any man, not Job's friends, not his wife and not Job. What's God's point, Abdul, when he asks 'Where wast thou when I laid the foundations of the earth?'"

Abdul looked up at me, concerned. "That we can't really understand God?"

"Good. And? Ariel?"

She let out a breath—this was the second time she'd been brought into the same world as Abdul. "And he's saying that if you weren't around when he made the world, then, like, you can't possibly understand what God does now. So, just give up trying and accept God. And that's totally what we should do. God has his reasons. We can't understand them. We just have to trust him no matter what. I mean I'm sorry that Job had all those shitty things happen to him but God had his reasons. And in the end he's better off than he started. So what's the big deal?"

"And all the children starving to death in the world? And the girls who are raped on their way to school? And the ten year old who is hit by a drunk driver? That's all God's plan?" Jane was trembling.

Abdul was nodding. Ariel turned coolly to Jane, smiled and said, "That's right," as if it were her plan not God's.

"O.K.," I said. "O.K."

After the bell rang and everyone else had left Gilad was still sitting at his desk.

"You O.K.?" I asked.

"Yeah," he nodded.

"Well come by if you want to talk, all right? I have a meeting now but I'm free later so . . . "

"You?" He interrupted me.

"Are you O.K.?" His face flushed. "I mean I'm sure you are," he said collecting his things and stuffing them quickly into his backpack.

"Yes. But thank you. Thank you for asking. It was hard to sleep last night. I woke up very early. But I'm fine. I'm fine."

He smiled at me, hoisted his pack over his shoulder and ducked out of the room.

* * *

I had an appointment to see the head of the school, Laetitia Moore, at ten-thirty and as I arrived she was walking the chairman of the board of trustees into the hallway.

"Always a pleasure to spend an hour together, Laetitia," he said smiling at her. Turning to leave he saw me, paused for a moment while his face fell from warm flatterer to cold businessman, and left.

She ushered me in and I sat down.

"So, Will. I understand that you didn't come to work yesterday. Is that right?"

I nodded.

"Can you explain why?" She wrinkled her forehead.

"They didn't tell you?"

"Something with the *métro*?"

"Something with the *métro*? Yes, I saw a man murdered. He was pushed in front of the train."

"Awful." She shook her head and spun a heavy silver pen on her desktop.

"I understand there was a student there?"

"Gilad Fisher."

"And he didn't come to school either?"

"That's correct."

"Did you tell him that would be O.K., Will?"

"We didn't discuss it. It wasn't really an option."

"Why was that?"

I looked at her for a moment and then said slowly, "Because there was a dead man under our train."

"And so the *métro* wasn't running," she said. She picked up a piece of paper and studied it. "The trains began running again at 11:45. So you decided you'd take Gilad to a café rather than return to school?"

"I didn't *decide* anything. It was a disturbing thing to see. To say the least. Gilad saw more of it than I did. He was upset. The *métro* station, as, perhaps you can imagine, was in chaos. I thought it best for both of us to leave there."

"I understand, but don't you think, Will, it would have made more sense to have brought him to school where he could have spoken to a trained psychologist?"

"What psychologist?"

"Cherry Carver, the school's psychologist."

"Cherry Carver? She's a math teacher. Why would I want Gilad talking to *her* of all people?"

"Cherry Carver is the school psychologist, Will."

"Since when?"

"Since the beginning of the school year."

"You're not serious."

"I am serious. She did a course over the summer. I'm sure an announcement was made."

"I didn't know."

"That's not what is at issue here. What is at issue is that you kept one of our students out of school because you felt that you were qualified to counsel him. You refused to provide a sub plan and you neglected all of your day's classes. It was bad enough that you didn't come to school. That you kept a student with you opens us up to a lawsuit. I'm sorry, Will, but what you've done is difficult to excuse. You have a responsibility to this school. You didn't fulfill that responsibility."

My hands were sweating. I could feel the rush of adrenaline. I stared at her. She stared back until eventually she spoke.

"I understand that you were trying to do the best you could for Gilad. I have to trust that you made the decisions you did with Gilad's best interests at heart but you have to remember that your job is to teach literature, not to counsel our students. Will? Do you have anything to say?"

I shook my head.

"Well," she said, "if you change your mind, you know where to find me."

"Is there anything else?"

"In fact there is, yes. The reason that Omar was here earlier is that he's concerned by one of your classes."

"Omar?"

"Al Mady. Mr. Al Mady tells me that Abdul feels very uncomfortable in your class. What is it?" She looked down at her notes. "Senior Seminar, is that right?"

"Abdul Al Mady is in that class, yes."

"Apparently, Abdul feels uncomfortable."

"I'm sorry to hear that."

"Is it true you've told the students that," she looked down at her notes, "that God doesn't exist?"

I laughed. "No, it is not. While I am confident that I'm a good teacher I don't feel that I'm in a position to comment on the existence of God."

"*Do* you believe God exists?" She gave me a stern look.

"You don't, honestly, expect me to answer that question."

She waved her hand as if swatting at a fly. "The point is that Abdul feels isolated, he feels that he's under attack, that his religion is under attack."

"I'm sorry to hear that."

"It's important, Will, that our students feel at ease in their classes."

I smiled.

"That's something that I feel very strongly about. We are here for our students, to provide a supportive environment, to make sure that they feel good about themselves, so that they leave here with high self-esteem. I want each of our students to leave our school with the sense that they are, in their own ways, special."

"And Abdul doesn't feel special? Is that Mr. Al Mady's concern?"

"Omar's concern, Will, is that Abdul is under attack in your classroom. That simply can't go on. Not with any student and certainly not with Abdul Al Mady. *Particularly* not with Abdul. In general, you need to be very careful when dealing with religion in the classroom. And above all, you can't challenge the faith of our students. Your role is to teach literature, not to question the existence of God."

"I disagree. I believe it *is* my role to challenge the faith of my students. In fact, I take it as my primary role—to question their faith in all things. It's impossible to teach literature, at least to teach it well, *without* questioning that faith. It also seems impossible that we should be having this discussion and yet here we are."

"Will, please. I've been an educator for more than twenty years. I hardly need a lesson from you. Clearly, a teacher should challenge his students. It is, however, one thing to challenge them and quite another to question their faith in God. You don't honestly believe that it should be you who questions their religion?"

"Within the context of a piece of literature? Of course I do. Those very questions exist already in the work I teach. Have you not seen my syllabus? The reading list?"

"I glanced at it this morning, yes. I saw that you're teaching *The Book of Job*. You have to understand that there's an important distinction, Will, between the questions posed in a text and those you pose directly to your students. You also teach *Macbeth*, Will. Would you have your students consider suicide or murder? These questions need to remain in the texts."

I shook my head. "I disagree entirely. Literature is irrelevant unless its questions have some bearing on the lives of the readers. You think a student who reads *Hamlet* shouldn't herself consider the idea of suicide? That when reading *The Book of Job* we shouldn't consider the existence of God? Or his logic? Or his nature?"

She stiffened. "Will," she said. "I will not permit you to use our classrooms to question God's existence, logic, or nature. It is one thing to discuss a character in a work of literature, it is quite another to treat the God of the Old Testament as a fictional character. This is dangerous territory. You have a moral responsibility to protect your students, to steer them through works of literature, to help them see clearly. That's it, Will. *That's* your job. No more."

"Laetitia, I disagree."

She drew a deep breath. "I'm afraid neither of us has time for an academic argument. Perhaps another time, but for now, you need to understand my position, which is to say the school's position. Simply put, you may not question your students' religious faith. For that matter, you may not suggest that they consider suicide or murder."

I laughed.

"Do we understand each other, Will?"

"I think so," I said, and left her office.

* * *

Mia and I sat together on the grass eating our lunch, the sun turning the poplars gold. A wind blew across the field and, for the first time that autumn, there was a sharpness in the air.

"Cherry Carver is the psychologist. She's the *official* school psychologist?"

"Apparently so. She claimed that there'd been an announcement."

"How does a school have a psychologist that the teachers don't know about? Who has *never* practiced psychology? Cherry Carver? Fucking Cherry Carver?"

"It's always for the kids. We're doing God's work. Don't forget that," I said, smiling.

"Speaking of which, I had a long talk with one of my new students. Marie de Cléry. Very sweet. Do you know that every day since the beginning of the year before she leaves she says, 'Thanks Ms. Keller. Great class, Ms. Keller.' She came by the office the other day to tell me how much she likes my class. *This* is why she stops by. To compliment me and to talk about the work? She stayed for an hour. She's my new favorite," Mia said beaming.

"That's good, it's good to have fans." I felt sick.

"No, I mean she's not like one of *your* panting groupies and she's not looking for grades. She doesn't really write all that well. She's fierce and interested. Everything we talk about, she tries so hard to understand and then when it clicks, she looks like she could cry she's so happy. It makes *me* want to cry. We're reading 'The Flea,' and today she had this expression on her face. I don't know, just total befuddlement, like she's in pain and then all of a sudden she sits up, her face bright and relaxed. She raises her hand, I call on her, and she says, 'Men are so pathetic.'

"The others start giggling but I know exactly what's happening and I smile at her and then all the other kids, none of whom have yet understood the poem, shut up, and Marie says, 'It's just another guy trying to get laid.' Of course she's right and she takes ten minutes to explain the whole thing to the class. It's not as if she's really literary but she saw the whole thing. While all the little SAT drones were looking for metaphors and similes, she just, click, gets it. 'All that to hook up with this girl? So lame. Just say what you want. Be a man,' she says. We spent the rest of the period talking about how men are pathetic. An excellent morning."

I loved the way Mia spoke about her students. I knew no one else who believed so certainly in what she did. I loved the way she taught, the way she worked for those kids, but I could barely look at her.

As we were finishing our lunches I glanced up to see Gilad walking back along the walkway from the cafeteria. When he passed, I waved.

He smiled and turned into the upper school building.

"That's him? The kid you kept from classes? The one you're morally bankrupting?"

I nodded.

"I've seen him around. He's alone a lot."

"Always. I like him. He makes me want to be good. I have a few this year. But he's at the top of the list. You should sit in on the seminar. It's great."

"Just let me know when."

"Any time."

"So what else, William?"

"Besides our new psychologist? And my recklessness? Well, let's see. There was the discussion of my responsibility not to challenge the faith of my students. Oh, and apparently she doesn't want me to encourage them to commit suicide."

"Well that's unreasonable."

"I think so. Omar Al Mady is complaining that Abdul feels uncomfortable, attacked, and persecuted and Omar, she called him Omar like we were all drinking buddies, isn't happy. I told her that it was my job to challenge the faith of my students, blah, blah, blah. But she was absolutely against it. No time for an academic argument, she said."

I heard a high pitched, "Mr. Silver!"

Julia Tompkins and Lydia Winton were walking toward us waving.

"Here's your fan club. We'll finish this later." Mia put her hand on my knee. "Will. Will." She shook her head. Then she smiled her sad smile, pushed herself to her feet and brushed the grass from her jeans. "I'll leave you to bask in their adoration."

She waved at the girls and headed back to the office. I watched her walk away across the field.

Julia dropped down next to me. "What's up, Mr. Silver? What's for lunch?"

She rummaged through my plastic bag.

Lydia, a year older and five years more sophisticated, sat down and looked at me purposefully.

"So, Silver, we've got a proposal for you," she said.

"Yeah? What is it?"

"Lit mag," Julia said. "Will you do it?"

"When?"

"Whenever you want to. Any day of the week after school."

"Except Friday. Obviously," Lydia said.

"Obviously," Julia rolled her eyes.

"Obviously," I said. "Find anything you like, Julia?"

She glanced one last time at the lunch bag, dropped it, shrugged and said, "Not really. And don't change the subject, will you do it?"

"Who else wants to do this?"

"Who knows?" Lydia had closed her eyes and turned her face toward the sun. "But believe me, Silver, people will sign up if you're the advisor."

"Totally," Julia laughed.

"But then, you know that already," Lydia said.

"I don't think there will be all that much interest but O.K. We'll do it on Wednesday afternoons. I'll get Ms. Keller to help. I mean if anyone shows up."

"Yay!" Julia punched me on the shoulder.

"I knew you'd say yes," Lydia said cocking her head to the side and smiling at me.

I stood up.

"Thanks, Silver," Lydia said.

MARIE

He didn't invite me back. I kept waiting but he never called. He'd smile at me in the halls and maybe he was a bit more flirtatious but barely. Just his condescending little smile. Sometimes I'd send him a text message. Tell him he looked good that day. I love when you wear that sweater, or something. And he'd respond. He'd tell me I looked good too. Fucking nothing. It drove me crazy. I didn't know what to do with myself. I started to feel desperate. I began to invent things.

I imagined he'd call or invite me over. Sometimes I'd write when I was drunk. I'd offer to come over but he'd say no. He'd tell me it wasn't a good time. I don't know. Maybe he had a girlfriend or something.

Please, I wrote. Please.

He said, Marie it's too dangerous. So I started sending sexual messages: I want you to fuck me. Then just as vulgar as I could come up with. I'd write and he'd respond. He'd always respond. Tell me what you want exactly. And that's when I started to lie. I'd tell Ariel that I was seeing him all the time. I started showing her the messages. I'd write them in front of her and we'd wait for his answers. Sometimes she'd write pretending to be me: Tell me what you want to do. He'd tell me and there was none of his tenderness in those messages. None at all. And he still wouldn't let me come over.

GILAD

I'd never read Shakespeare before his seminar. Before him I got by the way you do—CliffsNotes, SparkNotes, ClassicNotes. You read the chapter summaries, the analysis, you pretend. You don't ever have to read the thing. Shakespeare always felt like too much work to me. But the way he talked, the way he moved around the room, the guy was either a fantastic actor or he believed what he was saying. You just don't see that very often. Teachers in movies are always leaping onto tables and sacrificing their lives for their students and their love of literature but the truth is that you rarely, rarely take a class from a teacher who cares. It's just unrealistic. How many people could walk into a classroom year after year and weep for "Ode on a Grecian Urn"? That's why the ones who stay are so often some of the most depressing people you've ever met in your life. It has nothing to do with their age. They've stayed because of their disposition—bitter, bored, lacking in ambition, lonely, and mildly insane. With few exceptions, these are the people who are capable of staying in a school. This is what it takes to teach for half a life-time. The ones who care, who love the subjects, who love their students, who love, above all, teaching—they rarely hang around. Which is more or less what my mom told me in Senegal when Ms. Mariama lost her job.

"People think teachers are easily replaced," she said. "But that's only true of the bad ones."

Mr. Silver was the first person I'd fallen in love with. Not that there was sexual desire. Or maybe there was. It's hard to say. Any time you love someone that intensely, anytime you want to *be* loved that badly, sexual desire is always part of it. And when you're seventeen, eighteen years old, what doesn't have to do with sex? Not since Ms. Mariama had I felt *anything* for a teacher. I wanted everything for myself that he seemed to want for us—to live an involved life, to care deeply about something, anything, to feel the immediacy of time passing, to crave, to long. It didn't feel like rhetoric then. I still don't think it was. He believed it all, the whole thing.

When we began to study *Hamlet* that October I was excited about it. He'd asked us to read the entire play over the weekend. I liked that. It made me feel adult. It made me feel as if I *could* read *Hamlet* over a weekend. Sunday I sat in the sun in the Luxembourg Gardens in one of those green metal chairs with a thick scarf wrapped around my neck and the collar of my coat turned up. I read the entire thing through in one sitting. I took a break to eat a sandwich and then kept on going.

"Just go sit in a café and read the play," he told us. "Have a coffee. Take a pen."

He said these things as if they were obvious, as if they were what any normal person would do. But they weren't obvious things to most of us. Even if I explored Paris on my own, even if I sat by myself from time to time on the banks of the river, when he suggested them they were different, as if we'd be crazy *not* to listen. And so those many of us who loved him, we did what he asked. And we felt important, we felt wild, we felt like poets and artists, we felt like adults living in the world with books in our hands, with pens, with passions. And when we returned to school how many of us prayed he'd ask what we'd done over the weekend? Not only *if* we'd read but *where*.

And that's something.

"Just go sit in the Luxembourg Gardens," he said. "Get one of those nice free chairs, sit in the sun and read, watch the people, eat a sandwich, get out of your houses. Jesus."

And so I did. And I started wearing a scarf.

I looked forward to school. I fantasized about conversations we'd have. I prepared lines. I *wanted* to talk about *Hamlet*. There was nowhere else I'd have rather been.

* * *

From my notebook:

October 27

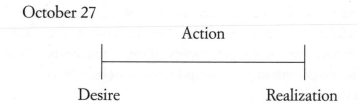

"So, what's the play about?"

He looked around the classroom. He raised his eyebrows.

Rick let out an impatient sigh. "So, it's about this guy Hamlet and how his . . . "

Silver interrupted him, "Tell me what it's about without telling me the story. I'm not interested in the plot. I want to know what the play is about."

"Yeah, O.K.. So it's about this guy—"

"Rick, tell me what the play's about."

"But it *is* about a guy," Abdul said to the empty notebook in front of him.

"I disagree," Silver said, shifting his gaze to Abdul.

"Whatever," Ariel said under her breath.

Without looking away from Abdul, Silver said, "Leave."

Abdul jerked his head up, his eyes wide.

"Ariel, leave the classroom."

"Excuse me?"

Finally he turned his gaze to her and said again, pausing between each word, "Leave the classroom."

We were silent. It was a kind of ecstasy. Aldo, with his mouth open, glanced from Ariel to Silver and back.

"Are you serious?"

He looked at her with an intensity and anger that I'd never seen from him. He was completely changed.

Ariel was a deep red. For a moment her usual sneer was gone. Then she looked at him as if she'd been betrayed.

"Fine, but I'm just going to say that this is . . . "

"Ariel," Silver snapped. "I'm not interested. Get out."

She collected her things, shaking her head, her mouth moving wordlessly. She looked at Silver for a moment as if sizing him up. There was an almost imperceptible smile on her face. Then she left the room, slamming the door behind her.

He waited a moment.

Lily broke the silence. "Dude," she said.

Silver walked over to the open window and looked out into the day. I remember watching him there, wondering what was next. The tall trees at the far edge of the field had turned and were lit up in the soft sunlight.

When he turned back he said, "You're wasting your time. If I were you, I'd run for it."

No one spoke.

He glanced up at the whiteboard and, as if just noticing the diagram, said, "That's the whole point, right there. That's the whole thing—the distance between desire and action, between what you want and what you do. That tension, that's everything. Can someone please explain to me what the hell I'm talking about?"

"The hardest thing is to do what you want to do," Hala said.

He nodded a dramatic nod.

"Or live the way you want to live," Rick said looking at the ceiling.

"Meaning?"

"That's the tension, dude!" Hala smacked her desk. "You know you want to do something but you can't get yourself to do it."

"Dude?" Silver grinned at Hala.

"Lily's fault. Sorry." We laughed.

"O.K., dude, why can't you get yourself to do it?"

"You're lazy," Colin said smiling.

"Wait, why would you not do something you wanted to do?" Abdul asked.

Silver squinted at Abdul. "Abdul, do you do everything you want to do?"

"Pretty much. Yeah."

"Do you talk to every woman you find attractive, Abdul?"

"I don't have to answer that. It isn't a decent question."

Hala let out a loud sigh.

"O.K., Abdul. O.K." Silver pushed himself off of the desk and looked around the room. "You're damn right," he said moving now, picking up the rhythm, "You certainly don't have to answer the question. Let's imagine for a moment that you're at a party. Let's take Colin as an example. Colin's at a party. He's standing in the corner. There he is. He's bored. He's thinking about leaving. And then, in walks the most beautiful . . . " Silver looked at Colin with raised eyebrows.

"Girl," he said laughing. "For sure a girl."

"O.K., in walks the most beautiful *woman* Colin has ever seen. Suddenly he's paralyzed. What is it about her? Her eyes? Her hair? He doesn't know. Oh, but she's magical, glowing from within, and so on."

Silver was pacing, loose and wild. Nodding his head, laughing. Drawing the scene, presenting this imaginary beauty with his hands, framing her, forcing us to see. "Here she is standing at the punch bowl. He wants to talk to her. He needs to talk to her. My God, she's beautiful. Look at her. All alone.

Look at those eyes. That sparkle. But. But, Colin? What's wrong, Colin? He can't cross the room. Oh he wants to, the pull is so, so strong. But no. Oh how he wants to. But he can't do it. The tragedy, the—"

"I'd cross the room," Colin said, arms crossed, chin raised, chest out.

"Oh, I'm sure you would, Colin. Because you're a *man*. But for the sake of argument let's just imagine, shall we, that you don't. Are you man enough to pretend?"

Colin smiled.

"So, why wouldn't Colin cross the room?" Silver stopped pacing, raised his eyebrows again and scanned the room, his hands upturned, shoulders shrugged. "Why?"

"Because he's a punk?"

Everyone laughed.

"And why is he a punk, Rick? What makes him a punk? You don't mind do you Colin? It's all hypothetical."

"No man, whatever."

"Did you just call me *man*?"

Colin met Silver's eyes, then after a pause, said, "Not you, just, it's just a figure of speech."

For a moment Silver looked angry and then it was gone. Was he kidding? Which was the thing about him. You never knew. Only *he* could push. You couldn't push back. Not too hard anyway. Everything turned on that tension. You never knew what you'd get.

"Rick?"

"He's a punk because he's a coward. Because he just can't get himself to walk over to her. To talk to her."

"Fear?"

"Yeah. Fear."

"Yeah." Pause. "Fear," Silver repeated. "That's the thing isn't it?" Searching the room for our eyes, digging for the unmitigated attention of every single one of us.

"Fear. *That* is what separates the hero from the common man. It's crossing the room. It's not complicated."

"So what? Heroes talk to girls?"

"Some of them do, Cara, I'm sure. But that's hardly the point. Come on. Push. Gilad, what's the point?"

I looked up from my notebook, my heart beating fast. "You do the thing anyway," I said.

Silver smiled his big smile. "Say that again."

"You do the thing anyway," I said louder staring down at my notes.

"You do. The thing. *Anyway*." Silver wrote it on the board. He leaned against the edge of his desk, crossed his arms and said again nodding as if we'd just discovered the answer to everything, "You do the thing anyway. Yes. Yes. You do it *in spite* of fear. You do the thing *anyway*. No matter what. Because you have to. Because you know it's right. Because you believe in it. Because by not doing it you're betraying yourself."

His voice was rising and he had us all. Even dim, defiant Abdul looked up to stare curiously at Silver as he came off the desk and was moving again.

"You do it because it matters and how do you know it matters?"

"Because it scares you?"

"Don't ask, Lily. Tell me."

"Because it scares you." She smiled.

"Because it scares you. You do it because it scares you. That's the core of it all. That's the center. That's how you know. That's the heart of the whole thing. The *heart*."

"So, I should jump off a bridge because it scares me?"

"Do you *want* to jump off a bridge, Abdul?"

"No, but you said—"

"Come on, Abdul. Think a little bit, O.K.? Come on. Give me something, man. Dig. Push, Abdul. *Push*. Let's go back to Hamlet. What does *any* of this have to do with this guy, Hamlet?"

And then the bell rang. Which is what often happened. He'd leave us with a question. The class would end and we'd file out wondering. We'd exchange knowing looks with one another. Even if we weren't friends, we were bound together somehow. And those of us who'd fallen for him always returned ready and nervous, wanting so much for him to notice us. And afraid that he would.

* * *

The days got shorter as October came to an end. Sometimes I ate lunch with Lily when she was around. Otherwise, I ate alone and read whatever he told us to read. I ran cross-country and usually stayed after school to train. I made some friends. Or I met some people to talk to anyway. Mostly though I kept to myself. I rarely saw my father. In the evenings I ate dinner with my mom at the small table in the kitchen.

All I wanted was to live the life Silver wanted us to live.

By then we'd read Sartre, *The Book of Job*, and *Hamlet*. The days were cold and beautiful and I tried to pay attention to them. I tried to pay attention to everything. Above all else it's what he seemed to want from us.

Waiting for the *métro* those mornings, I always hoped he'd see me. I dressed for him and stood with a book open, waiting. When I heard someone descending the steps onto the platform I'd furrow my brow as if immersed in my reading.

I saw him from time to time. He'd slip into a different car, or sit with his back to me. Those days I never had the courage to speak to him. Sometimes we'd walk from the *métro* to school together. I waited for him to ask me questions but he asked very little. He was warm. He smiled. Always said good morning.

"Good weekend?" he'd ask. "Doing O.K.?" He meant after

what we'd seen together. But when I thought about that man dying in front of me I thought mostly of how it brought us to Au Petit Suisse. Put me there at a table with Silver. How he'd taken care of me. How I thought maybe I even took care of him. The event itself didn't haunt me the way the school counselor thought it should. I'd been obligated to meet with her once a week.

During those walks with him from the *métro*, he'd sometimes ask about the reading: did I like it? Was it interesting to me? I gave generic answers while I searched for something intelligent and original—witty, spontaneous observations that would reveal my maturity, the wisdom beyond my years. They never came.

And then, as we entered the gates of the school, I'd lose him to the morning crush.

* * *

On November eighth he handed out copies of *The Stranger*.
From my notebook:
November 8, 2002
Stranger—read for the weekend.
Saturday—Place de la République—*manif*.
And then one of his handouts clipped and pasted onto the page:
From the *NY Times*—1968—John Weightman:

As a white African, he evolved a kind of solar paganism fraught with melancholy. "Nuptials" celebrates the union of the young man with the natural beauty of sun, landscape, and sea. "The Wrong Side and the Right Side" signifies that life, even when lived to the full in the ideal circumstances of the Mediterranean, has its undercurrent of sadness. "There is no love of life without despair about life" is one of the aphorisms coined by Camus to express this view. He means that even in moments of intense lyrical appreciation—for instance, when bathing in the summer sea with his girlfriend, like Meursault, the hero of *The Stranger*—he is conscious of some inherent tragedy in the universe.

That was a Friday. He read sections of the essays aloud to us. Ariel wrote across her stapled packet, "Are we still in elementary school?" She turned it and showed Aldo who grinned his moron grin, lank hair hiding his face.

But the rest of us listened. Even Colin had stopped smirking. Over the last month he had taken on an air of near-violent intensity. He spoke less and less, scratching away, paying careful attention. He hadn't returned to class for a week after he'd walked out. And then one day he was back, ten minutes late. Silver said nothing, only nodded at him as he walked tentatively into the room. As the days passed he began to concentrate. He leaned in toward Silver. I thought it was an act at first, a provocation. But it wasn't. He'd made some decision and since his return there'd been only one incident, when we discussed *Hamlet*.

Silver had written on the board, "Alexander died, Alexander was buried, Alexander returneth into dust. The dust is earth; of earth we make loam; and why of that loam; whereto he was converted, might they not stop a beer-barrel? Imperious Caesar, dead and turn'd to clay, Might stop a hole to keep the wind away, etc.—Ham 5.1."

"Why?" he'd asked us, "is Hamlet talking about Alexander and Caesar?"

"We all return to dust," I said without thinking and then looked up, surprised to hear my own voice.

He smiled at me. "Yes," he said. "Go on, Gilad."

"It doesn't matter who we are. Were. We die. We disintegrate. We fill holes. That's it. That's all."

"And so?"

I looked down at the quotation I'd copied on my page. When I looked up I met his eyes. He seemed to be studying me, curious. I felt the warmth of affection, of pride. Chosen. To be looked at that way by him. I couldn't speak.

"And so," this was Colin, "nothing matters. But we have to live anyway. That's the problem. Nothing matters but we have to live anyway. Even though we end up in someone's ass, we have to live anyway."

Laughter.

"I was with you up to the ass part," Silver said.

"He says," Colin was flipping fast through his copy of the play, his cheeks red. "Here! 'To what base uses we may return, Horatio! Why may not imagination trace the noble dust of Alexander, till he find it stopping a bung-hole?'"

Silver smiled at him and nodded his head. "Look at the note, Colin. A bunghole is a hole bored into a barrel."

Ariel laughed too loud. Colin narrowed his eyes.

"However, the point you make remains. You said that nothing matters but we have to live anyway. Go on."

There was a silence. Then, "No matter who you are or what you've done in your life, you end up dirt." Colin turned to Ariel and said, nearly spitting, "We all end up dirt."

"Exactly," Rick said to himself.

"Except," I said.

Colin turned to me. We looked at each other for the first time that year. I was struck by his anger, the rage in his eyes. It frightened me. And it made me jealous.

"Except?" Silver asked.

"Except it isn't totally true."

"Why not?"

"Because we don't *have* to live. That's the whole point.

That's Sartre. That's Shakespeare here. That's the whole question. To be or not to be. That's the question. To live or die. To die. To sleep."

Colin looked at me. His eyes softened, he nodded his head. "You're right," he said.

"*They're* right," I answered daring a fraction of a smile. He relaxed. Nodded his head again in approval.

"And so we choose what to do with our lives. We do even if we don't. We choose by not choosing. That's what Sartre says, right?" Hala, who'd fallen quiet those last weeks, was leaning forward again. "We either kill ourselves or we do something with our lives. That's it. Those are the choices."

"Totally," Lily said chewing pensively on a braid.

Jane laughed and looked up at Silver.

Rick nodded to himself. Abdul stared at his desk nodding in silent dissent. Cara, her head back, studying the ceiling, asked, "So that's what he means by absurd? I mean that's the absurd thing? We die anyway but have to live."

"Totally," Lily said smiling at Cara. "Totally."

Cara looked at Silver for confirmation but he only gave a slight grin.

It felt to me then, for all of us who were on his side, who loved him, as if something important had happened. It had little to do with the philosophy, such that it was, and everything to do with Silver, with having pleased him, with having become, in some way, adult. It was a feeling of adventure and family.

"What crap," Ariel said.

We all turned to her, all of us except Colin who fell still, staring into the middle distance.

"Killing yourself isn't an option. It's wrong. Come *on*. Life isn't as simple as that. There's instinct, there's, human, I don't know, you don't just like, what? Jump off a bridge? You can't live as if suicide is a real option. It's *such* a stupid idea. I mean how can you sit there and swallow that crap?" She looked around the room as if the question was one she actually wanted answered.

"That's a good question, Ariel," Silver said. "Can anyone answer it?"

I took a breath to speak.

But then Colin turned to her and said, coldly, slowly, emphasizing every word, "Shut your fucking mouth. Shut the fuck up."

Silver stood up and said sharply, "Colin," and then again, "Colin, stop now."

His eyes dark and mean, Colin turned toward Mr. Silver as if he couldn't understand why he'd been interrupted. What was there to say? What could Silver want at that moment?

"Colin, go," he gestured toward the door with a slight nod of his head.

No one moved or spoke. The two of them locked eyes. Then Colin stood up and turned to Ariel. Her eyes were bright with anger. She was impossibly pretty. Colin looked directly at her. I saw her face. I saw her weaken, saw her eyes reflect something like fear. I watched the blood beating through her long neck.

"Colin, now."

"You're nothing," he whispered in that thick, comical, menacing Dublin accent. "Nothing, right."

He took his things and left the room, closing the door quietly behind him.

WILL

I taught seminar last period that day. They'd read Camus's lyrical essays over the weekend and I was looking forward to the discussion. I hadn't had time to prepare and I imagined that perhaps reading Camus again might provide me some sense of calm.

Gilad and Colin were sitting next to each other when I walked in and when I saw them together I felt an immediate thrill of paternal pride. Gilad, who'd been so isolated since the beginning of the year, might now have a friend. And Colin, who'd pushed me so hard, was so deliberate in his belligerence, had, nearly overnight, become interested almost to the point of obsession, in every word I spoke. Seeing the two of them sitting side by side buoyed me. And it wasn't only those two: there was Lily and her braids, her natural demeanor, her easy laugh. Hala, who could have passed for a thirty-year-old lawyer, whip smart, sarcastic, and funny, her pure disdain for Abdul. Cara, her dark cynicism, her silence, her detachment, and her unabashed disregard for assignments, long black hair in her eyes, her occasional flashes of interest. Jane, having abandoned her purple hair and angel wings, rising up through the mire of adolescence. And Rick who'd been so aloof, had taken to crushing and precise retorts to Ariel's various commentaries and diatribes. Suddenly there was an enthusiasm for the class, for me, for philosophy, and there was an alliance, a building sense of unity as if, in a moment, all the pieces had fallen into place.

There had been a day, weeks before, when I'd stopped talking altogether, when, in discussing the last act of *Hamlet*, I'd let go entirely. They took off, making connections themselves, listening to one another, pushing one another, laughing. There was that rare upswing, a growing excitement, entirely driven by interest, by their own enthusiasm for the play. They were beyond the classroom, they were sailing as I stood in the corner. I could have slipped out the door, could have left them to it. But I wanted to watch. I wanted to see it. It was the best thing, better than any love, any passion, any meal. It was the truest, rarest, sweetest thing I knew and for whatever it was, five minutes, ten, we were all out there together. They carried me.

But Ariel couldn't allow it. She cut it off. We were all fools. She claimed to be offended by the notion of suicide as a viable choice, as a choice at all. And the whole thing fell apart. Colin lost his temper. That kid, a straining mass of muscles. He might have hit her. It didn't seem impossible in the moment. I had to send him out. As much as I sympathized, I couldn't let it go.

Later that afternoon I walked with Colin around the field.

"You understand right?"

"Yeah."

"You're sure?"

"Yes, sir."

"O.K., I wanted to make sure. While you didn't choose the best way to say what you felt, I do know you weren't the only one in the room to feel the way you did."

We passed a group of kids sitting in a circle on the grass, notebooks open.

When we were out of earshot, Colin began, "She—"

But I interrupted him. "I know. She can be difficult and she makes you angry, but at the very least you have to tolerate her. Ignore her if you can."

He nodded. "It's not that, sir. She's, look, you have to understand. I think you should know. I mean you were good to me. You gave me the time. You did what you said. I kept expecting to be called into the office. But, you know, nothing happened, no one came. I liked it, I liked coming to class because I wanted to. It made a difference."

"I'm glad for that. You were brave to challenge me, to walk out."

He nodded, "Thanks for the chance. Seriously, Mr. Silver." He paused. "The thing is that you should know she hates you."

I laughed. "I'm used to students hating me. It's part of being a teacher."

He shook his head, "No, but I think this is different maybe. She really hates you. She says things about you."

"Things like what?"

"You really want to know? You want me to tell you? I think you should maybe just know that she says them. Know that she's a . . . she's mean."

She's mean. It was an uncharacteristically innocent thing for him to say. I stopped walking and turned to him. It was the first time I didn't trust Marie.

"If you don't want to tell me, don't. But I appreciate your being concerned."

In class, Ariel had lost some of her bravado, spoke less, seemed frightened by Colin. She never dared to look in his direction. Instead, she brooded, ignored everyone, even Aldo, abandoning him to a hostile majority. He had nowhere to turn. He'd been too long Ariel's loyal ally, muttering and smirking his way through the semester. And Aldo didn't dare solicit Abdul Al Mady's company, for Abdul moved in a social world far beneath his own.

So at the beginning of November it was among those kids, during that seminar, that I felt a familiar sense of strength, a faint sense of the future. Most of them were with me. The other three were hamstrung. They'd have to sit silent or come around, and really I didn't need them. The rest of us, we were making something, we were alive in there. It was all I had, and I suppose I imagined then, foolishly, that it was all they had too, and that it would be enough.

GILAD

S ilver had tried to continue the discussion, end it with some kind of normalcy, but when the bell rang we were for once all grateful. Ariel had gone quiet. The rest of us too. On the *métro* home that afternoon I tried to understand what it was that made her fight him so hard. It made no sense to me. All her friends were doing their best to have him notice them.

As far as I knew there'd been no repercussions after Colin's explosion. Since then we'd begun saying hello to each other in the halls.

"What's up, man?" he'd say.

It made me feel stronger. I found intimacy in those exchanges. I looked forward to them.

And now, weeks later, a cold Friday afternoon, the poplar trees across the field waving in long, slow gestures, their yellow leaves full of sunlight, I listened to Silver read the week to an end:

"'Space and silence weigh equally upon the heart. A sudden love, a great work, a decisive act, a thought that transfigures, all these at certain moments bring the same unbearable anxiety, quickened with an irresistible charm. Living like this, in the delicious anguish of being, in exquisite proximity to a danger whose name we do not know, is this the same as rushing to your doom? Once again, without respite, let us race to our destruction. I have always felt I lived on the high seas, threatened, at the heart of a royal happiness.'"

He looked up.

"Don't follow along. Look out the window. Close your eyes. But listen." I did and it felt to me that I wasn't alone.

"From Albert Camus's 'The Sea Close By'" he told us and then repeated a line obviously memorized, "'I have always felt I lived on the high seas, threatened, at the heart of a royal happiness.'"

And then uncharacteristically he used the first person: "I've always felt this way."

I opened my eyes and when I saw him I thought he was going to cry. He wasn't acting. He couldn't have been. It would've been impossible.

He looked out the window, then returned to his yellowed paperback. "'There are women in Genoa whose smile I loved for a whole morning. I shall never see them again and certainly nothing is simpler. But words will never smother the flame of my regret. I watched the pigeons flying past the little well at the cloister in San Francisco, and forgot my thirst. But a moment always came when I was thirsty again.'"

There were only a few minutes left before the bell. He looked, after reading this last line, the same line he'd read on Monday, wistful in a way I'd never seen him.

"What was it that Camus was thirsty for?" he asked. "What are you thirsty for?"

Hala raised her hand, but he shook his head, "Have a good weekend," he said. "And read."

* * *

Friday after school I walked with Colin to the *métro*. It wasn't planned. We simply didn't avoid each other. I'd seen him before, walking ahead, lighting a cigarette as he passed through the gates, calling a casual good-bye to the guards. Countless times I'd walked behind him among other kids wandering along the street, laughing and shouting, free from school. We poured out of there. The joy of temporary freedom. And I didn't mind those walks alone, among but not with the rest of them. I liked watching and not participating. It made me feel stronger, and for months I was convinced that I wasn't lonely. I also liked to be alone because I thought it might endear me to Silver, whom I'd occasionally see walking with other kids, waving, exchanging jokes with other kids as he made his way quickly away from school.

Perhaps he'd find me more interesting if I were alone, pensive, pondering great ideas—a young philosopher, an independent mind. But at best, he patted my shoulder in passing. See you tomorrow, Gilad. See you tomorrow.

So that Friday, finding myself side by side with Colin as we left the school, I was surprised by how grateful I was for his company.

"Hey," he said.

"Hey."

Then I was as they were. Which is to say with someone else. All those months of isolation, all those months alone, and then here was Colin.

He offered me a cigarette. I shook my head.

"I should quit," he told me. "Silver's always giving me shit about smoking."

"Really?" I felt a shot of jealousy.

"Yeah, you know. We had this talk one day where he said how I thought I was a rebel for smoking. Like, I was all tough smoking cigarettes. And then he gives me this whole lecture about how smoking is totally *not* rebellious, about the tobacco industry or some shit. He was fucking right too. As always. So anyway, I'm going to quit. I'm trying to." He laughed.

I waited for the jealousy to pass. The sense of betrayal even. As if, all this time, Silver had been mine alone.

I said, "You know the day that guy was killed, Silver took me to a café. We spent the afternoon there."

Colin looked at me, "Yeah? That must have been intense, man. Seeing a guy like that. Fucked up."

"Yeah it was."

"What'd it sound like?"

"I don't know. It was. To be honest? The noise was hidden by the sound of the train. It was fast. Then there was nothing. Then there was crunching. Like branches being broken in half. But all of it was kind of far away. Like it was underwater. Or I was. I don't know."

"Fuck," he said and glanced at me sideways. He seemed impressed.

We walked quietly for a while, Colin blowing smoke. We walked down the stairs into the *métro*.

"So you going to this protest on Saturday?" he asked as we slumped down into two forward-facing seats.

"I guess. You?"

"I was thinking about it."

"We can go together if you want," I said, after a long pause.

He nodded. "Yeah, O.K. Sure, that'd be cool. All right. Cool."

We exchanged numbers and he got off the train at Nation. He raised his chin at me as the train rushed on. For the first time since arriving at ISF, the fact that it was the weekend meant something to me.

* * *

I opened the door. My mom was crying and in the midst of an angry sentence when I walked into the room. My father, in a black suit, red tie in hand, white shirt opened at the collar, stood close to her.

"Gilad, go to your room, please."

He didn't look at me but instead kept his eyes on my mother, whose expression softened as she saw me.

I pushed the door closed. It was the first time I'd seen my father in weeks.

"Gilad, go to your room."

I didn't move. I said nothing. And then he turned to me angrily. There was a faint sheen of sweat on his forehead.

"I'm not messing around, Gilad. Either get the fuck out of the apartment or go to your room and stay there."

They were both looking at me, my mother's eyes pleading.

"Gilad, are you fucking deaf?"

"Don't talk to him like that." My mother spoke to the floor. Whatever fury there'd been before I walked in had drained from her. Now this pathetic effort to defend me. He ignored her. I couldn't move.

He took a step. My father, a few inches taller than I was, thicker, came forward, careful, hesitant even, as if he didn't want to leave my mother alone where she was.

"Gilad," he said again, "I'm not fucking around. This isn't your problem. Get out."

I met his eyes and didn't look away. I felt as if I might dissolve. I needed to keep looking. If I broke the whole thing might fall, whatever balance there was, whatever was keeping us all still. I couldn't look away.

"Touch him and you'll never see me again," she said. This time in a stronger voice, gathering whatever she could of herself.

And then, still looking at me, he took a quick step toward my mother, swung his right arm backward, and struck her squarely across the face. It was as graceful and precise a stroke as every sweeping backhand I'd ever watched him hit on tennis courts around the world. There was a dull, flat sound. My mother gave a slight contained cry, a fast expulsion of breath. And it seemed as if his eyes had never left mine. He opened his mouth wider as if to speak. At first, nothing, and then, softly, "Do you understand me, Gilad?"

I wanted, with everything in me, to leap at him. I could see it. Feel my fist crushing his jaw. Throwing him through the door. Through the window. Cutting his throat. Tearing him apart. His blood on my knuckles. I felt myself rising to action, building, it was coming, I was tight, I would move, take him by the throat. I'd murder him.

Instead, I looked away toward my mother who was pretending to be concerned rather than afraid. She raised her head slightly and we looked at each other. Then I looked above her head, through the window. There was cold sky behind her. The branch of a plane tree coming and going in the window. Trees beyond bending in the gusting wind. A piece of wire dangling from a rooftop, twirling behind the double-glazed glass. I saw Sacré Coeur, silent and pale in the far distance, pasted to the sky.

"Gilad, get the fuck out."

Ignoring him, I looked back at her. A spill of red rising across her right cheek, flecks of blood on her lips. Her eyes dull.

"I'm sorry," she whispered to me. And again, "I'm sorry."

In that apology I found my escape. It wasn't my fault. It wasn't my job.

So I left them there.

* * *

That night I stayed in my room. I pissed out the window into the courtyard below. I read. I walked back and forth. I held the door handle. Imagined opening it. Breaking down their door. Cross the fucking room. Dig down. Push. Go.

But I was a coward. I stayed where I was. I looked out into the night and put it all away. I looked out my window and knew that Silver, somewhere in the city, was in his apartment. He'd be reading. Listening to John Coltrane or something. Or at his desk, grading papers. Writing poems maybe. The light low, a beautiful bare-shouldered woman reading on the couch. There he was living his honorable life. I saw it clear as anything.

I thought about the morning, about meeting Colin. The next day we'd fight. We'd fight against something important. Tomorrow we'd be brave.

* * *

I woke up very early and left. Their bedroom door was closed. In the weak morning light, everything looked as it always did, the pillows on the couch returned to order.

And then one day you live in France.

I stepped out onto the rue de Tournon. I ran to Boulevard St. Germain and turned east. I kept running. It was a little after six and the streets were quiet. Cafés were opening, tired waiters lining the sidewalk terraces with chairs, smoking their morning cigarettes. I ran past the street cleaners dressed in green, sweeping away last night's trash. I ran to the Pont de Sully. I ran until I was exhausted. I opened my coat and began to walk, the chill morning air cooling the sweat on my chest, my face, the back of my neck. I crossed the bridge and stopped to watch the sunrise over the dull industrial buildings to the east. I walked up Boulevard Henri IV until I came to the Place de la Bastille and took a table at the Café Français. Waiters were still arranging chairs when I sat down. The wind was very cold. I ordered a crème and a croissant. The waiter didn't speak. The coffee and milk came in separate steel pitchers, both scalding hot, and the croissant was still warm. I hadn't eaten since lunch the day before. I ate very fast and then, remembering Silver, poured the coffee and milk very slowly.

The first thing I thought after my hunger had subsided and the coffee began to brighten me was that he'd approve. He'd like that I was sitting there alone, so early in the morning, paying such careful attention to simple, beautiful things. Paris morning, coffee, milk, pitcher. His imagined approval made me feel as if it would be O.K.. Whatever was wrong, it would be O.K..

They had nothing to do with me. My mother had made her own choices and she continued to make them. What did that have to do with me? She'd married him. She'd given up. She stayed. My life was my own, I'd soon be free of them, and my anger, my new easy conviction, propelled me into the day.

I opened my backpack and found *The Stranger*. How proud he'd be of me sitting alone in the cold morning, the book on the table next to the remains of my breakfast. All alone, the day unfolding. I moved the book with its uncracked spine as if arranging the subject of a still life, moving a cup this way, an ashtray the other.

From my backpack I took out the French *poche* version I'd bought at L'Ecume des Pages. I would read it first, make clever observations about translation and how much more I'd enjoyed the novel in its original language.

Aujourd'hui, maman est morte. Ou peut-être hier, je ne sais pas. Mother died today. Or maybe it was yesterday, I don't know.

Those first words. I was wide-awake. It's embarrassing even now, after all the time that's passed. How many teenagers had fallen for that book by the time I found it? But I didn't know and I suppose that's to his credit. He never told us and I didn't think to ask.

The whole scene had been done—the Gauloises and the black turtlenecks—but to me then it was a secret gift handed to us one Friday afternoon at the beginning of our lives.

I read the way you read when you're young. I believed that

everything had been written for me, that what I saw, felt, learned, was discovery all my own. I read for hours without rest. That man who barely flinches at the news of his mother's death—that morning he let me abandon my own mother, to leave her, without guilt, to her own life, her own choices.

When I looked up, it was nearing eleven. I ordered an omelette and another coffee. The café had begun to fill. I was surprised to find people around me, reading newspapers, chatting. I was part of that place, part of that moment, one Saturday morning. I didn't think about the night before. I shut it out. Camus was mine that day. Silver had given him to me. Meursault and all the rest.

I walked up Boulevard Beaumarchais, hands deep in my coat pockets. Close to Place de la République, there were dark blue police vans lining the Boulevard du Temple, hundreds of them it seemed, riot police strapping on their armor, smoking cigarettes, drinking coffee from thermoses, preparing themselves calmly for battle. I saw one brushing his teeth, spitting into the gutter. I took my time so I could watch them.

Those men were strong, waiting for a violence certain to arrive.

Later they'd use their batons, their fists. They'd be attacked, barraged with bottles. They'd throw people to the ground.

There were already signs on the statue of la République. People milled around, waiting for the protesters who would march en masse from Bastille. The wind had picked up and was blowing leaves across the square. Groups of kids hung around wearing the Paris street-tough uniform of the day— nylon track suits, pants tucked into white socks, fanny packs slung around their waists, and little caps worn backward, or with hoods thrown over their heads. A crowd was gathered at the base of the statue looking up at some boys who'd climbed halfway to the top and were hanging a large banner—"Anti-Bush/Anti-Guerre." There were girls sitting on top of a bus stop drinking beer. Pretty students with peace signs painted on their cheeks wandered through the crowd handing out anti-globalization stickers. Vendors sold *merguez* from a makeshift grill.

It felt like a carnival, the crowd so young. They were jubilant. I'd never been to a protest and I was thrilled to be in the midst of so much enthusiasm, all those kids, not much older than me, singing, chanting, and hating the United States together. A girl wearing a military cap, her hair in pigtails and a T-shirt—fuckUSA—smiled at me. When I smiled back she pushed a T-shirt into my hands and insisted I put it on. I tried to refuse but she was too beautiful. I pulled it over my head. She kissed me on the cheek and danced into the crowd.

There were banners everywhere. Signs plastered to walls, bus stops, and lampposts. People were pouring in from every direction. Traffic had been stopped and the wide streets were a mass of protesters. There was a constant buzz of sound and motion and all of it seemed to be accelerating as I made my way across the *place* to meet Colin. In my new T-shirt I felt connected, part of the wild crowd around me.

They raised their fists in the air. "FuckUSA," they chanted, laughing.

"*Oui mon vieux*," a bearded man said as he passed.

"*Non à la guerre, non à la guerre*," people sang.

"*La paix, pas le sang, la paix, pas le sang, la paix, pas le sang.*"

There was the faint sound of far-off chanting and the steady beating of drums.

Colin came up the steps, out of the *métro*, lighting a cigarette. He grinned when he saw the T-shirt.

"In the spirit aren't you, mate?"

"Find the right girl and you can have your own."

I put my hand out to shake his but he slapped my palm twice, and then offered me his fist. I followed his lead and touched my knuckles to his. He laughed his sharp laugh and shook his head at my clumsiness.

"Don't get out much do you?"

We'd started walking and I looked straight ahead. "I'm out all the time," I told him.

"Yeah? I never see you clubbing, man. Or at the *Champs*."

"Not really my thing."

"That's cool. So where do you go?"

"I don't know, just out in the city. Walk around. Go to cafés. I listen to music sometimes. You know."

He gave me a look and nodded his head as if coming to understand something. "You're a bit of a fucking loner then aren't you?"

I shrugged my shoulders. "Maybe," I said. "I guess."

"I mean that's cool. Most of those fucking cunts at school aren't worth your time anyway. That's sort of Silver's trip, you know? Being fucking in it. Out there. Connected and shit. Not wasting your time with fucking idiots, doing fuck all."

The way he spoke made me nervous. Walking with him I felt polite, mild. Colin spit. Flicked his cigarettes into the street. Swore. Talked loudly. He was tight and angry and I was drawn to him, envious of his disregard for the world, his easy swagger. I was also embarrassed by him, by his crassness, the amount of sidewalk he took up, the volume of his voice and even by his clothes. He dressed like a kid from the *banlieue*, those white nylon track pants tucked into his socks. He had the same bravado, the same arrogant gait.

"Yeah," I said. "I guess that's what I'm trying to do, you know. Like he says, 'live bravely,' fight against, I don't know, whatever." I glanced over at him sideways as we walked, expecting him to laugh. I felt like a fraud, but he just nodded.

"It *is* brave. The way you're doing it. Going it alone. That's a hard fucking life though, man. What about girls? You have a girlfriend?" He looked at me and then said, "You're into girls, right? You don't have a fucking boyfriend, right mate?"

"No," I told him. "No boyfriend."

"And?"

"No girlfriend," I said.

"Fucked up, man. I know there are chicks at school who'd fuck you. You're that mysterious kid. They love that shit. Even if you have some of that Columbine thing, man, chicks fucking love mystery."

I laughed.

"So what's up?"

I shook my head. "I don't know, really. I'm just. I don't know."

"What?"

"I don't know. I just want to do something else. I'm tired. Like I'm a hundred years old. Like I was born bored. Bored of people anyway. I don't know. I'd like to meet someone wild. Interesting."

Which was half true. But despite my desperate, painful, adolescent sexual desire, I never had anything to say to the girls who smiled at me. I was in a constant state of longing. My body hummed with need and all of that yearning, that stifled desire—to fuck, to tear the apartment to pieces, to escape, to break my father's jaw—the only relief came while I was lying in bed at night. There, with my eyes closed, I'd draw an image from my memory—one of those ISF girls running to class, or lying in the sun, or raising her hand—and I'd masturbate angrily until I fell asleep. Often it was Ariel, late in the afternoon, the school empty. I'd bend her over Silver's desk and fuck her violently from behind. Or little giggling blond Julia, always talking with Silver out on the field, she'd be on her knees in front of me in the bathroom, her hair in my fist, or Marie de Cléry with her famous breasts heavy in my hands. There was an invariable violence to those fantasies and with every ejaculation came the slight release of rage, the faintest relief from anger. In my bed, in the shower, even once in a bathroom stall at ISF, I'd grit my teeth and masturbate until the skin was raw and still the erections would return again and again.

"Silver's fucking *alive*. I'll bet that guy is crazy wild," Colin said.

I nodded. "He's the first person for a long long time that's really got to me, you know? He's always in my head."

"He's the only reason I'm here today. No offense, but last year, I wouldn't have been here. On a Saturday? Sorry but fuck that. I'd still be asleep."

As we arrived on the *place,* a massive crowd was moving slowly up the Boulevard du Temple. All along were cheering spectators. We pushed in and stood at the edge of the sidewalk where we watched as wave after wave of protesters came up the boulevard. Various groups marched behind their banners—socialists, Union des étudiants juifs de France, other student unions, Democrats Abroad, Marxists, communists, Christians for Peace, Iraqi refugee groups, Hezbollah, Americans Against the War. There were girls wrapped in rainbow peace flags who danced unaffiliated. They held speakers above their heads and sang "Imagine."

I watched stern-faced men and women marching behind bright-yellow Hezbollah banners decorated with green fists clutching AK-47s. Bouncing university hippies flashing peace signs followed behind and I felt I was in the midst of something important, but I was chilled when I saw those yellow flags, having been taught early in life to fear Hezbollah, and to hate it. Standing so close, I felt immersed in a dangerous and exotic world. I was part of a true rebellion. All of us were together there in the greatest city in the world, all of us from everywhere, raging against the world's bullies. Raging, engaged, participating in something. We were there. Present. Alive. I knew he'd be proud of me. For chanting *"Non à la guerre, non à la guerre,"* my fist in the air. And my parents? If they'd known I was cheering as Hezbollah marched past, they'd have been furious.

American diplomat father, Jewish mother—with all our time spent in Arab countries, the ever-present anti-Semitic undercurrents, and then those years in Israel. They'd have been furious. Cheering was an ecstasy. Louder and louder I chanted *"Non à la guerre, non à la guerre,"* until the refrain took on a violence all its own. Colin leaned against a lamppost, smoked and watched the scene, keeping his eye on a group of hippie girls dancing braless a few yards away.

"Really into this, aren't you, mate?" he yelled.

I turned to him, my throat raw, and nodded. "Got to be engaged," I told him, mimicking Silver.

"Fuckin' right," he said, bowing his head and putting his fist in the air.

Flowing from Boulevard du Temple, the protesters spilled out onto the place, which served as a sort of estuary. The order the boulevard provided to the marchers was immediately lost as they flowed outwards around the statue of la République. Banners, which had earlier been drawn tight, drooped. Now red-shirted communists filtered among dancing rainbows. Eventually the last straggling protesters arrived, followed by city workers methodically picking up garbage, spraying the asphalt clean. And behind them a slow parade of CRS was flanked by their creeping blue vans.

People distributed leaflets, chanting, screaming into megaphones. What had been a single massive protest had become a sea of smaller ones. We found a man selling sausages, bought our lunch, and ate sitting on a curb.

"Who *are* all these people?"

"Don't know, man." Colin shook his head.

"They're so *into* it."

"I bet most of them are just here for the fucking party. I mean look at those girls running around with their rainbow flags. In a couple years they'll be looking for a job in a bank just like all the rest of us. Maybe those hairy fucking Marxists are in for the long ride, and those guys with the AK-47 flags, but mostly? Come on, it's a street party."

"Those guys were Hezbollah," I said, watching members of the Union des Étudiants Juifs de France form a small group across the street. "Anyway, maybe you're right, but I've never seen anything like this, man. Look at how young most of them are. They're like us. They're out here."

The students wore white t-shirts with the words *Juifs Contre la Guerre* written across their chests. They were talking, laughing, leaning on their signs. They had a sort of glow, which I saw then as one of purpose and confidence. It was the same look I saw in a thousand people that day. Faces that seemed to radiate certainty, a passion for their cause, they were out there doing what they believed in. Living their beliefs, assuming responsibility, acting in accordance with their desires. They were all the things I was sure I was not. They were all the things that Silver expected us to be. As the crowd grew, there was a slow rise in volume, megaphones raised to the sky, chanting from across the *place*. I watched the faces, the backslapping camaraderie, and felt, yet again, challenged by a world that existed outside of myself, by a version of life I was not part of, a version of life I saw as infinitely more pure than my own, and by the growing sense that it was a life I'd never possess.

I wanted to say something like this to Colin. I wondered if those people I saw as young, fiery, passionate examples, tempted him, seduced him the way they did me. I turned and was about to speak when, a hundred meters away, I saw Silver forcing his way through the crowd. I watched him weave in and out, moving in our direction. He stopped on the other side of the gathering Jewish student union to wait in line for a sausage.

"Silver's here," I said not looking away.

"Fuck off, where?"

I nodded toward the sausage stand. It thrilled me to have

this new power. To watch him, as Colin joked, "in his natural habitat." I was fascinated. I watched the way I'd watch him waiting for the *métro*. But it also felt as if I were somehow betraying him. Suddenly the day felt delicate and fragile. I held my breath, waiting to see what he'd do. I expected something horrible, or I feared it.

To our right there was loud laughter. A small group of tough-looking kids was standing in the street. Poor and from the suburban *cités* you saw all over Paris. They were the angry, swaggering kids Nicolas Sarkozy would, three years later, refer to as *racaille* and promise to clean out of France. They hung around *métro* stations, stole purses, harassed single women, rode the RER, mugged young kids, and fueled the xenophobia that was rampant throughout the country.

I felt a shift in the mood of the crowd. People slowly began to move away and I had a clear view.

"This isn't good," I whispered to Colin.

"No, mate," he said, straightening.

Sitting with him I felt protected. He was small, but he could fight. I once watched him break the nose of a kid who'd tripped him in a lunchtime soccer game. I'd seen him take on Ariel. But this was something different, another level. This was not school. It was the world.

I watched several of the kids tie patterned kaffiyehs around their faces as they began to taunt the Jewish students across the street.

"*Sales Juifs*," they yelled, spitting on the ground for punctuation.

"*Allez vous faire foutre, putains de Juifs.*"

The Jewish students didn't react at first. They ignored the taunts and pretended not to hear. But nearby the crowd went quiet. Now there was a pocket of meanness amidst wild celebration. My heart was pounding.

"*Espèce de sale Juif, je vais me faire ta sœur,*" a gangly kid in a Gucci T-shirt yelled, his face hidden behind a red-and-white kaffiyeh.

There was little reaction. They stiffened at the vulgar taunting but otherwise continued to talk to one another. We stood up. There was too much violence in the air.

Nothing happened.

And then I watched as a short kid in a Nike cap hurled an empty beer bottle against the opposite curb. It exploded and sent shards of glass flying into the small group across the street. Finally one of them spoke. A tall guy with short curly hair turned around and said, "*Ça suffit.*"

"*C'est à moi tu parles, connard?*"

I'd forgotten briefly about Silver, who appeared just to the side of the students. He stepped quickly through the crowd to the curb where, perhaps for the first time, he was confronted with the source of the yelling. He held a sausage in one hand, his lips slightly parted as if he were on the verge of speaking.

Silver's presence calmed me and while I felt less afraid I also knew, in the moment I saw him there, that I was a coward. I knew it absolutely. He'd come to remind me, to show me what I was.

What kind of person are you? he'd asked us in class. I was the kind of person who stayed still, who remained motionless while every bully in the world stormed forward in a blur of violence. I stood humiliated, paralyzed, and trembling with anger. I turned to those idiot kids. I stared at them.

I would walk to the tall one with the scarf around his face. I'd step off the curb while all the rest of these frauds with their placards and slogans did nothing, stood waiting for something to happen. I'd defend myself. I'd defend all of us.

I put on an angry face, hoping he'd glance my way and see my outrage, see that I was on the edge of action. Two of the kids in kaffiyehs stepped off the curb into the street, one of them holding a metal bar in his hand.

They were only a few feet from Silver, who stood still on the edge of the curb.

The tall student from the Jewish union said nothing. A few others stood at his side. One of them, a young girl, sexy I'd thought earlier, with long blond hair tied back in a loose ponytail, screamed, "*Vas te faire foutre!*" Her face was flushed and she was shaking. Someone grabbed her wrist and told her to be quiet. She pulled her hand away and faced the two men.

The one holding the metal bar said, grinning, "*Quand je te sauterai, tu parleras moins fort, salope.*"

Someone in the crowd drew in a quick breath of horror. I looked at Silver. He wouldn't allow this, I thought. The tall student looked out at the silent crowd facing him and shook his head, disgusted.

The guy with the bar turned as if just then noticing his audience. He spread his arms out, raised his shoulders. Looking for a challenge, daring one of us to respond. When he turned to me, I looked away.

He swiveled, searching, a smirk on his face, gauging the people surrounding him. The tall student stepped off the curb and walked toward the man with the bar who, when he saw him coming, swung it evenly, hitting him hard in the ribs. The student doubled over, holding his hand to his side.

Silver stepped into the street and yelled, "*Arrête!*"

The man with the bar looked at him, surprised. "*Quoi? Qu'est-ce que tu vas faire?*"

They stared at each other. For a moment no one moved. Then with two hands he pushed the bar against Silver's chest, throwing him backward where he tripped and fell into the crowd. He took a step forward with the bar raised. Silver flinched, covering his head with his arms. The guy spit, tossed the bar to his friend, raised his fists and said, "*Viens, tapette.*" Silver, staring back blankly, his face red, camera hanging over his shoulder, never raised his fists.

"*Viens.*" He beckoned. "*Pédé, va!*" he said, and spit in Silver's face.

Cheek wet, he didn't move.

There was a strange silence, a radiating pressure. I remember thinking how odd it was that all of this was happening in the open that way, in dazzling daylight, all of us held down by fear.

The man turned to look at us again, and when he did the tall student came from behind and punched him hard in the side of the head.

And just before everything exploded, before the students rushed onto the street trying to protect their friend, bleeding on the asphalt, before the CRS came tearing through the crowd, dressed like storm troopers in full riot gear, before the short one who'd thrown the bottle grabbed the blond girl by the hair and threw her to the ground, I saw Silver wipe the spit from his cheek and disappear into the crowd.

Colin grabbed my arm and pulled me away. The CRS came from all sides swinging batons. There were skirmishes throughout and whatever sense of peace, whatever illusion of order there'd been an hour before, had turned now to frenzy.

Later a truck would arrive with water cannons to knock rioters off their feet. Metal tear gas canisters landed with hollow rattling clicks and the air filled with white.

It seemed to me it was the moment Silver turned away from us and disappeared that the Place de la République fell into chaos.

* * *

That evening I sat on a bench in the Square Laurent Prache not wanting to go home. I thought about Silver teaching "Dulce et Decorum Est."

"Read this," he said, "so as not to forget there's a war coming."

"'Drunk with fatigue; deaf even to the hoots / Of gas-shells dropping softly behind,'" he read. "What's interesting here? What surprises you?"

Hala knew immediately. "Softly," she said. "He says, 'softly.'"

"So, why is that interesting?"

"Softly. It's like gentle, calm. It doesn't fit. You have all of these horrible images—'froth-corrupted lungs' and 'vile, incurable sores' but then there's this one word in the whole poem that's, I don't know, peaceful."

He smiled at her and nodded. "So why does he do it?"

"The gas is a relief," Colin said.

"How?"

"It saves them. They get to die, man. 'Men marched asleep. Many had lost their boots / But limped on, blood-shod. All went lame; all blind;' I mean who wants to live like that? Look, they've been marching with their dried-blood shoes, they're totally broken, and they've got this stupid idea that they're doing something honorable and here's a way out, this canister."

"Like an angel," Lily said. "Landing softly to save them."

"Good. Great, yes. Anything else?"

"The green?" Jane ventured.

"Go on."

"'The misty panes and thick green light, / As under a green sea, I saw him drowning.' All that, it's, I don't know, peaceful too. The green, the sea, the panes, it feels calm and slow and even the drowning seems, I don't know, like a relief, like the speaker is almost envious of his escape."

"What escape? Death?"

"Yeah," Cara said, looking up from beneath her black hair. "Like he's lucky to die. He doesn't have to make a decision, he doesn't have to deal with stopping, he just gets to die. No choice. No choice at all."

It went on like that. We consumed that poem. We were, by the end of class, furious at the war, at the hypocrisy of government, or whatever it was we were furious about. It didn't matter. It was that ecstasy of legitimate anger that mattered, and the thrill of doing it ourselves, unraveling a poem, so many of us in it together and Silver so proud, pacing around, driving us forward.

Sitting beneath the trees now in St. Germain-des-Prés I kept hearing those tear-gas canisters clattering against the asphalt at République. Such a vacant sound. People running in fear. So much chaos. I couldn't comprehend the distance between who we were that day in his classroom and who we were now.

I read from his packet of Camus essays.

It happens that the stage sets collapse. Rising, streetcar, four hours in the office or the factory, meal, streetcar, four hours of work, meal, sleep and Monday Tuesday Wednesday Thursday Friday and Saturday according to the same rhythm—this path is easily followed most of the time. But one day the "why" arises and everything begins in that weariness tinged with amazement.

It was nearly dark and I was very cold. There was a man lying on a bench opposite me, wrapped in an old blanket with a wool hat pulled down to cover his whole face. I watched him and imagined I had the courage to spend the night there in the park. I'd never go home. Just take a breath and fade away. No phone calls. I thought about the man I'd seen pushed in front of the train. I'd pasted the article into my notebook. Christophe Jolivet was dead in a second. I thought about the sound of the train hitting his body and how it was so different from the one the metal bar had made against that kid's ribs.

Il n'y a qu'un problème philosophique vraiment sérieux: c'est le suicide.

In pretending that I had the courage to sleep in the garden with this faceless man and Picasso's bronze of Dora Marr, I also imagined I had it within me to kill myself. But I didn't have the courage for either. And I was perfectly aware, even at seventeen years old, how ridiculous I was sitting in St. Germain-des-Prés clutching Camus pretending to contemplate suicide. I was freezing and soon I'd go home.

For a moment, I thought I might call Silver. Maybe he'd take me in, let me sleep on his couch for a while, until I figured things out. But of all I'd seen that day, all I'd proven to myself about my own character, what haunted me most was that single image: Silver turning away, his hand rising to his cheek to wipe the saliva from his face. What had I expected?

When he came forward and cried out, I felt such relief. This would be the end of them, the end of all of it. I knew Colin thought the same. In that moment, he was ours. Righteousness had arrived in a sea of ugliness.

But there was nothing more. What he had to give he gave. It was an inch more than the rest of us, a brief scream. *Arrête.* And then there was nothing but a diminishing wave of inertia leaving Silver standing there in the street, mute, as we all were, with fear. I saw him stumble backward, refuse to fight, and turn away. Gone.

I couldn't call him. There was nowhere to go but home. Nowhere I had the courage to go.

A round man in a long black coat opened the garden gate. He walked to the bum lying on the bench and gently shook his foot until the man woke, pushed his cap above his eyes and sat up. He gathered his blanket, picked up a pack from behind the bench and limped silently out of the garden. The man in the coat glanced up at me.

"*Le jardin ferme, je vais vous demander de partir monsieur, s'il vous plait,*" he said.

I nodded and stood up, pulling my backpack over my

shoulder. He held the gate for me and smiled as I walked past. "*Bonne soirée*," he said, sliding a key into the lock.

I went home. The apartment was warm and smelled of roasted chicken. I was hungry and the warmth of the place, the lit candles in the living room, the Bach cello suite playing on the stereo all made me grateful, in spite of myself, to be home. I'd imagined slipping into my room undetected. But now I listened to that doleful, keening cello, my cheeks warm with cold. The great strength I imagined I might possess upon my return home was lost.

The music ended. I heard a faucet come on in the kitchen, the sound of water falling into the sink. Then it stopped. Footsteps. I breathed slow shallow breaths and watched the kitchen door. She walked out into the living room, her right cheek red and swollen, the beginning of a bruise rising below her eye. There was a spot of dried blood on her lip. Her hair was down around her shoulders. She wore jeans and her long gray turtleneck sweater. She crossed the room. I knew she'd replay the album. It was János Starker. She'd play it when I couldn't sleep or when I woke from nightmares. "Magic music to slay monsters," she'd say.

When it began again—those slow, deep chords—she turned and saw me.

"Gilad," she said, raising a hand to her cheek. Her eyes were dull but she was lovely in spite of herself.

"Hi," I said. She came closer and seeing her like that—so small in her thick wool socks, sleeves pulled over her hands, her lip bloodied, her eyes dead, there was nothing of her left to hate.

"Is he here?"

She shook her head looking at me.

"Where'd he go?" I whispered.

"Left. He was leaving for Berlin tonight anyway. He's gone."

I dropped my bag on the floor, stepped forward, and wrapped

my arms around her. When she began to cry I held the back of her head with my hand.

"You're so cold," she said. "You're freezing cold."

I was quiet and she kept her cheek against my chest. I looked out toward Montmartre and Sacré Coeur white on the hill.

After a while she said, "Are you hungry?"

I followed her into the kitchen. There was a roasted chicken on a cutting board and a bowl of sautéed potatoes on the counter. She carried both to the table. I brought plates and silverware. She sat across from me and poured two glasses of red wine from an open bottle.

"I'm sorry," I said.

"Gilad, you have nothing to—"

"I do. I'm sorry I left you like that. I'm sorry I couldn't do anything. That I didn't do anything. That I haven't ever."

"Gilad, it isn't for you. It should be me, I'm the one. You're just . . . " She began to cry again.

"I should. It *is* for me. I'm just like he is."

Her expression changed quickly. There was, in an instant, a return of color to her face. "You," she said, her voice shaking, "are nothing like him. Nothing. Listen to me. It isn't your fight, it isn't your job to take care of your parents. Anyway, you can't expect to find this courage you want so badly. It won't just *come* all at once. You'll discover how you're going to be brave. Your father," she shook her head, "he's a bully, Gilad. You'll never be that. Never. You may be afraid of him but that fear doesn't make you a *coward* for Christ's sake. It's your *father* who's a coward. Not you, do you understand me?"

I looked up at her, her eyes narrowed. She was angry and it was a relief to see that she was still alive. She was trying so hard to pull herself up, doing her best to be my mother.

"I don't understand how you could have allowed that. Why you followed him, how someone like you, how you could . . . "

"End up like this?"

I nodded.

"Someone like me? Life sweeps you up, Gilad. Things happen fast, you forget to pay attention. Or you stop paying attention. You lose that thing."

"What thing?"

She shook her head. "I don't know exactly. People used to tell me when I was young that I didn't know what I was capable of, that my intelligence was limitless, that I could do anything. Which I've come to realize is true in both directions. I never imagined that I was capable of this life. It would have seemed impossible to me when I was younger, but God do we surprise ourselves. They never tell you that what we surprise ourselves with may be disappointment. No one ever told me that perhaps one day I'd find myself capable of disappointing my son. But here I am." She took a sip of wine, looked up, and touched my cheek. "I know you think I was this wild-spirited artist, carefree and full of confidence, but I wasn't. I was just a kid wandering around in Paris with no idea what to do. I was smart, O.K., fine, but I had no real strength, no real conviction. I was tired and out of money and I thought I'd have to return home and become, what? I don't know, an art teacher? Christ, I'd have to return home to all those people I swore I'd never be, to lives I despised. Then I met your father and he offered me an easy way to live what seemed like a glamorous life. You can't imagine the pleasure I felt telling my parents and my friends that I was moving to Africa. I felt cosmopolitan, so accomplished, as if I'd *done* something. I pretended that it had nothing to do with your father. That's a very limited kind of courage, Gilad, following someone else's life. Anyway, I didn't plan to marry him. I was caught up in creating a story, and now, well, that's what I've got, a good story. It's just a good story."

I listened and ate my dinner.

"The thing is you have to fight the whole time. You can't

stop. Otherwise you just end up somewhere, bobbing in the middle of a life you never wanted."

"So what? That's it? You've given up? This is it for you? You'll stay with a man who's barely here? And when he is, he beats you?"

She was crying.

"I'm sorry." I looked away for a moment. "Mom, I just don't accept that this is it, that you're going to spend the rest of your life alone in expensive apartments pretending to be happy."

We sat together in that kitchen for a long time. I told her about the protest, about Hezbollah, about the silent crowd and the metal bar. About Silver.

"At least he said something," she said.

I shook my head angrily.

"What do you want, Gilad? What do you *expect* of people?"

I looked up at her bruised face, her bloodied lip. There were slight lines around her eyes I hadn't noticed before. It was late. She was exhausted. She looked back at me as if she wanted, more than anything else, an answer to her question.

* * *

I'd promised myself I'd never do it again but on Monday I took the school bus with all the others. I didn't have the energy for the cold walk from the *métro* and anyway, that morning I was short on principles. I had Silver first period. I thought about skipping it. About skipping school in general. But then I suppose I was expecting some sort of explanation. How he'd snuck around the back and broken the guy's neck. Something.

He began class with an uncharacteristic lecture:

"In 1958 the *Front de Libération Nationale*, Algeria's revolutionary party, attacked and killed four French policemen in

Paris. Maurice Papon, then the chief of police in Paris, organized retaliatory raids against the Algerian community throughout the city. He rounded up thousands of Algerians and threw them in, among other places, the Vélodrome d'hiver and the Gymnase Japy, which by the way, is still there, just off boulevard Voltaire if anyone's interested. Do you know why I mention these two places in particular?"

He was cold that morning, humorless, acid, sarcastic, and unfamiliar. I remember Hala squinting at him, her face revealing a combination of confusion and concern. She wrote quickly in her notebook. Whatever play had been there on Friday, whatever lightness, had gone.

"I mention them because they'd both been used in 1942, sixteen years earlier, during *La Rafle du Vel' d'Hiv*. Anyone have any idea what I'm talking about?" He looked around the room. He was fierce. "Abdul? Any idea? Ring any bells?"

Abdul nodded.

"Yes? Good. So tell us about it, tell us about *La Rafle du Vel' d'Hiv*."

He kept nodding but shrugged his shoulders. "I don't know."

"No?" Silver said, "No."

"I do." This was Hala who ordinarily would have enjoyed seeing Abdul's ignorance revealed, but she was upset, and glanced worriedly at Abdul as he went on nodding, tapping his fingers on his notebook. Silver leaned back against his desk. He crossed his arms and raised his eyebrows at her.

She looked at Silver angrily. "*La Rafle du Vel' d'Hiv*. The police arrested thousands of French Jews."

"Yes. Good." He went on. "Of those twelve thousand Jews, more than four thousand were children. Pétain used both the Vel'd'Hiv and the Gymnase Japy as detention centers. The Jews were kept there until they were sent to Drancy. And from Drancy they were sent to Auschwitz where most of them died. So now we jump forward to 1958 when, instead of Jews, the

French police begin rounding up Algerians, throwing them into the Seine, torturing them, and so on. This continues through 1961, when the FLN resumes its attacks on the French police, eleven of whom are killed in less than two months. As a result, anyone who even looked Algerian was fair game—people were attacked, arrested, drowned, and tortured. Men had their hands tied behind their backs and were thrown into the river for appearing Algerian. Maurice Papon called a curfew and made it illegal for Muslims, not only Algerians, Papon said 'Muslims,' to be out in the street between eight-thirty and five-thirty. The FLN called for a peaceful protest and in October of 1961 thirty thousand people marched against the curfew. Throughout the city, the police shot into crowds and flung people into the Seine. Most famously at Pont Saint-Michel, not far from where many of you spend your Saturday nights drinking. Two hundred people were killed. All of them Arab.

"Ten years ago we discover Papon collaborated with the Nazis. He was convicted of 'complicity in crimes against humanity' and sentenced to ten years in prison. But that's another story. Why am I telling you this?"

He looked around the room, daring one of us to respond.

"Why? Because Sartre, living in the midst of all of this, having once been a prisoner of war, spoke out in support of the FLN and an independent Algeria."

He hesitated for a moment and shook his head. "Never mind his failures during the occupation."

He went on. Fierce.

"Sartre wrote angry articles against the mistreatment of Algerians and the racism endemic throughout France. He was called a traitor and anti-French. Accused of treason, he received death threats and yet he did what he'd been doing for nearly all of his adult life, he continued to write. Sartre's apartment was bombed. He kept writing. And then again it was bombed, this time entirely destroyed. But he kept writing anyway."

No one spoke.

"What's the point, right? You tell me. What's the point? Abdul? What's the point?"

Abdul ran his fingers back and forth across his page. Silver looked around the room.

"Anyone?"

"I suppose, sir," Colin said looking blankly at the backs of his hands, "the point would be that we should do the same. We should fight against things like that. Corruption and oppression and the like. Despite fear. Do the thing anyway. Would that be right, sir? That if we don't, sir, it's all just writing, it's just theory like you told us, just, like you said, 'words on a page.'"

He spoke without emotion. Silver looked at him steadily and nodded.

"The thing is, sir, about all this fighting back and standing up, we'd need to have courage, right? We'd need to be able to find the courage to do the fighting. And if we can't, well, we're just stuck here watching the world go by, like you told us, watching the world go by, like everyone else, like you said, 'cowards.'"

"That's true," Silver said nodding, his eyes narrowing.

"Would that be like you, sir?" Colin asked finally looking up and meeting Silver's eyes.

"I'm sorry?"

"Someone like you. A fighter. Someone who, like you said, has the courage," Colin flipped through his notebook until he found the page and read, "'To travel the distance between desire and action' is what you said. That's what you told us about courage, sir. That's what separates the brave among us, 'the ability to travel the distance between desire and action.' I've got it right here. October 27."

Colin raised his notebook from the desk and held it open for Silver who nodded and said, "Yes, Colin. I think that's right. But what's your point here?"

"*My* point, sir? I was answering your question. It was *your* point we were discussing. The point you were making about Sartre and the Algerians and the Jews and all that."

"Yes, Colin," Silver said, cold, "but what does it have to do with me?"

Ariel had been watching Colin with renewed interest.

"I guess I'm just wondering if all this courage you want us to have, I just wonder, sir, if it's the kind of courage you have yourself. I mean if I can ask that, without being rude."

Silver glanced away from Colin and out to the field where a light fog had filled the space between the bare poplar trees and the low buildings of the school. He seemed to contemplate the question and then, turning back, he said, "I've never pretended to be an example, or to have more courage than anyone else. I've never claimed to be braver or stronger or more capable of action than anyone else. But then, that doesn't really answer your question does it? Do I have the kind of courage Sartre had? That's the question, right?"

Silver said this quietly. He seemed deflated, melancholy. The anger and icy cadence gone.

"Yes, sir."

"No, I don't think I do. Why, Colin? Why the question?"

After a long pause he shook his head. "Nothing, sir. I was just wondering."

"How can you say that?" Hala asked, staring at Silver incredulous.

"What? Say what, Hala?"

"How can you claim you're not an example?"

"Hala, I didn't say that, I didn't say that I wasn't an example. I just never *argued* that I was. Or should be."

"Mr. Silver," Jane said exasperated, her cheeks red. "As a teacher, I mean, as a teacher you *are* an example. I mean, even if you never said it, even if you never explicitly said it."

"That's the point, in your role, you have an a priori responsibility, a priori as Sartre says." Hala went on, nodding at her allusion. "You may not *claim* to be an example, but you *are* nonetheless. You are anyway. You don't get to decide how people see you. And you know, right? That you *are* an example to a lot of the students at this school, Mr. Silver? I'm sorry, and I don't mean to be disrespectful, but you don't get to choose."

Silver took a deep, slow breath. "Well, Hala, I don't know. I don't know how many people really see me as an example. But that's for another discussion. I *do* play a role in how I'm perceived. The clothes I wear, the things I say, the way I say them. I, as we all do, cultivate an image. I'm no more pure than anyone else. What is far more important is that all of these people who supposedly consider me an example, they also make a choice don't they? They decide to see me one way or another, right?"

I watched Silver carefully as he spoke. As I studied his eyes and watched his mouth move, the way he picked at the dead skin on his thumb, my heart beat faster and harder. I felt something rising in me and when he came to the end of his question, I let out an exasperated breath.

He turned to me, his eyes sad. He seemed so tired.

"Gilad? Something you want to say?"

I glanced at Colin. He was looking at me.

"Mr. Silver, I just, I wonder if you believe all of that." I felt nauseated and my face was hot. I wiped my hands on my jeans. He narrowed his eyes. He seemed surprised by my question.

"What do you mean, Gilad? Believe what?"

"I mean, do you actually expect that a tenth grader, someone fifteen or sixteen, you expect that they make this decision? That they're capable of deciding how to see you? Of really, fairly judging you, judging your, I don't know, your authenticity? They make a decision to see you one way or another? That you, I don't know, share the responsibility of the thing? You and the student? That it's equal?"

We all looked at him and waited for an answer. We barely moved, all of us unified in our anticipation. Silver looked at me, and this time I held his gaze. He turned to Colin. The tension was terrible.

Abdul coughed. Silver turned to him. "What do you think, Abdul?"

Then I was angry, I felt a surge of rage. How dare he rely on Abdul.

Abdul rocked back and forth, his nervous nod taking over his whole body. "I don't know. I'm not really sure."

"About what, Abdul?"

"I don't know. Yeah, you're a teacher. So you're responsible, yeah. You have this job. It's your job."

Silver nodded impatiently, his slight gesture bordering on the ironic. "Anyone else?" he asked.

I raised my hand now. It was a formality I'd long ago abandoned. My own ironic gesture. Silver turned to me. He'd walked to the window and opened it and was leaning with his elbow resting on the frame, looking away from us. I felt the cold air chill the sweat on my neck. I was grateful for the cold, thankful that he'd opened the window and again, I felt sympathy for him, warmth, and I wondered briefly if perhaps he'd opened the window for me, seen my face flushed, the sweat on my forehead. I wished for it. And again I felt as if I were betraying him.

But I kept my hand raised.

"You don't have to," he began still looking away from us. Then he turned back to the room, shook his head and said, "Yes, Gilad," in the same tone he might have used with Ariel.

I was holding my notebook open. "Can I read you something? It's Sartre."

He nodded and I read, "'What do we mean by saying that existence precedes essence? We mean that man first of all exists, encounters himself, surges up in the world—and defines himself afterward.'"

Again, there was nothing. No response. No noise. No shuffling of papers, or the sound of pen pushing across paper, no whispering. I looked at Silver, who raised his eyes at me and said nothing.

"'Encounters himself.' You said that to encounter yourself, it's the point when you suddenly understand, when you begin, when you no longer can pretend that life is otherwise, when you realize the truth of the world. That's more or less what you said, I think. That's how I have it." Again, I spoke with the faintest edge of irony and in false deference.

"Yes," Silver replied. "I think that's right. Yes."

"And you think that your students, not to mention all the other kids here who you don't teach, but who know you, who see you around, who *hear* about you. You think they've *encountered* themselves?"

When he didn't answer, I returned to my notebook and read aloud the Camus passage I'd read on Saturday in the Square Laurent Prache:

It happens that the stage sets collapse. Rising, streetcar, four hours in the office or the factory, meal, streetcar, four hours of work, meal, sleep and Monday Tuesday Wednesday Thursday Friday and Saturday according to the same rhythm—this path is easily followed most of the time. But one day the 'why' arises and everything begins in that weariness tinged with amazement.

I read slowly with a confidence and strength of voice I'd never possessed in his class, or, perhaps, ever in my life. I expected to hear noise, Ariel whispering to Aldo, Lily giggling, but no one made a noise.

"You think, Mr. Silver, that those sophomores you teach, that they're weary? That for them the why has arisen?"

I was sweating again despite the cold air filling the room.

Silver nodded slowly, watching me carefully, as if confirming something to himself. He smiled and this time it was something else, pride perhaps. And in that smile I felt satisfaction, pleasure, happiness, all because he'd been impressed, because he was pleased with me. He smiled and nodded and closed the window and returned to his desk, to his usual place.

"I do," he said. "Yes. However, you clearly disagree, Gilad. You've certainly done your homework."

I shook my head. I was no longer angry. He'd disarmed me.

"We have, sir, we've done our homework, Gilad, and I," Colin said.

And then Ariel began: "What crap. What total crap. What a cop out. You think you can do what you want to do? That the responsibility is on us? On the students? You claim, like, what? That it's all just equal? That you have no more power than we do? No advantage?"

Silver had pushed himself off the desk and was standing facing her. She had gone so red it seemed the blood was seeping into her eyes.

"Ariel, watch the way you speak to me, I—"

"Why? Because you're the teacher? And I'm the student? You can do as you like, right? And then you make it all O.K., justify it all with this bullshit?" She flipped her copy of *The Stranger* onto the floor where it landed with a dull thump on the worn brown carpet.

Silver took a step closer to her desk. His face revealed, along with anger, panic and perhaps even fear. "Ariel," he said, his voice falling an octave, "close your mouth."

She stood up and stuffed her notebook into her bag. She fastened the straps, dramatically wrapped her long white scarf around her neck and then, when she was prepared to leave, she raised her eyes to him. At her full height and in her winter boots, she was taller than he was. She looked powerful, full of conviction, so certain of herself, not a hint of hesitation.

"You're a fake, Mr. Silver. Pathetic," she said looking directly at him. "I know, Mr. Silver. I've known for a long time."

She came out from behind her desk and stepped forward so that they were, for an instant, very close to each other. And as she left the room she passed by him so closely that a strand of her hair trailed across his shoulder.

WILL

I thought I might be inspired, get caught up in the whole thing. All that chanting. Angry slogans. It was a gorgeous day. Sunshine. Cold. People everywhere. It felt good to be out in the city. But the spirit of the crowd felt wrong. Too many people out for blood. It got uglier and uglier as the protesters came to a stop, filling the Place de la République. The girls, faces painted with peace signs, had all gone home. The students singing "Imagine" had left. There were Stars of David and swastikas side-by-side on the same banners: "*Sionisme = Nazisme.*"

I stumbled into a crowd gathered near a group of stands selling *merguez*. I bought one and stood watching a group of Jewish students being harassed by some drunken kids. I looked on along with the rest of the crowd. I stared at the kid who was conducting the whole thing. I wanted to kill him. The people standing in front of me left and I found myself on the edge of the curb, on the same level as the students, and I continued to watch from behind my sunglasses. Then I saw Gilad and Colin. They looked frightened, boxed in by a growing crowd. I knew they were there because of me. Participate in the world, I told them. That tired speech. And here they were participating.

Stand up and show your students what it is to be brave, what it is to act. I'd do it for them the way I might someday do it for my own children. In spite of fear, I'd protect them. I'd be the one to step out of the crowd.

I didn't think they'd seen me. I stood motionless, pretending to focus my energy on that belligerent kid. And when he hit the student with his bar and he raised it again, I stepped off the curb and told him to stop. "*Arrête!*" I said. And there I was in the middle, with quiet all around, and I could see him, every detail. I said nothing else. He saw instantly that I *had* nothing else.

Gilad and Colin saw it too. Their hypocrite teacher standing alone in the street, praying that "stop" was enough and knowing it wouldn't be.

* * *

Saturday night had come and gone. It was nearly one in the morning. I got out of bed, dressed and went out.

I walked toward the Seine away from the noise of the rue de Buci and farther down the darkening street. I turned through the small arch and stepped out onto the cobblestones in front of the Institut de France. I couldn't bring myself to walk onto the Pont des Arts. Lights on the water. Drunken students playing their guitars. Instead, I sat on the steps at the edge of the *place,* cast in a mean orange light.

There was nothing to think about. There was nothing to do. Nothing was next.

Couples walked along the *quai.* Some turned to look up at that golden dome, snapping photographs as they passed.

Somewhere in a bound album, I thought, I'll be the shadow in the corner.

I walked home, up the dark street where I passed a couple pressed together against a wall. When I arrived in front of my building, her message came.

It was the beginning of November. There were six people in

Bar du Marché next door. A local drunk was sitting alone in the entryway of an apartment building across the street. He cracked his head against the door. Over and over again he snapped his head back. As hard as he tried he couldn't seem to knock himself out. I was holding the telephone.

I watched him fling his head back one last time. His skull thudded against the wood and he fell forward, where he stayed.

I thought of walking over to him, of taking his head in my hands, of sitting next to him, allowing him to rest against me. Maybe later, I'd tell him. Maybe some other time.

The light in the stairwell was out. I turned upwards in the dark.

From my window, I could see Pauline in her kitchen washing dishes.

The wind had picked up and was blowing through my apartment. I was grateful for the cold. I watched as Sébastien wandered in wearing a pair of jeans. He wrapped his arms around her as she moved a sponge methodically around a plate. Soon they switched off the lights.

I saw myself moving away through the crowd.

And then in the dark waiting for Marie.

"O.K.," I wrote. "*Viens.*"

* * *

By then, the mornings were dark. I arrived at school earlier than usual. First one in, I made a pot of coffee and then stared out the window while the machine choked to life. It was November and still the sky was clear, the sun just coming up over the trees. The grass was white with frost.

When Mia arrived, I poured her a cup of coffee. A small boy in an orange parka ran out into the middle of the field. His were the only tracks. Together we watched him lie on his back, spread his arms and legs, and beat a snow angel into the frost.

Then he stood and ran back into the school.

* * *

That afternoon we ate lunch together on one of the benches outside the cafeteria. The air kept its morning bite. She shivered and wrapped her scarf tighter around her neck.

"How was your weekend?"

"Pretty horrible really."

"Did you get my messages?" She looked away and watched some students playing basketball.

"I did. I'm sorry."

"You could have called me back. I thought we were supposed to see a movie."

"I should have called."

She sighed and shook her head. She began to speak. But I stopped her, saying sharply, "Mia, I'm sorry. I said that. I should have called. Let it die, O.K.?"

"Why was it such a hard weekend, then?"

I tried to describe a widening darkness, the sensation of something collapsing. It was a relief to say it.

"Hang on," she whispered and looked over my shoulder.

"Hi, Ms. Keller. I'm so sorry to bother you but I was wondering if you have time to go over my essay this afternoon. I looked for you in the office but this is the first time I found you, so I'm really sorry but . . . "

"It's fine, Marie. Calm down. This afternoon, I'm free the last two periods."

She was standing very close to me, her hip inches from my arm. I kept my eyes forward.

"Yeah. Thank you *so* much. That's great. I'll come last period because I have History the period before but I'll be there as soon as I'm out. I know you're busy, so thank you, thank you, thank you."

Mia laughed. "Relax, Marie."

"Hey, Ms. Keller, remember in *Gatsby* what Daisy said about her daughter, 'The best thing a girl can be in this world, a beautiful little fool.'"

"And what, now you *agree?*"

"Please. O.K., I've got to go. Thank you, again. See you later."

As she turned from the table her arm brushed against my shoulder. I could smell her as she went, and that touch went through me.

"Sorry," Mia said. "That girl's great, I adore her, but she never stops. You know her?"

"I've seen her around."

"Marie de Cléry."

"'The Flea.'"

"She's great."

Kids were spilling out of the cafeteria doors on their way to class. They carried half-eaten bags of chips, candy bars, cans of Coke.

"So, how was *your* weekend?"

"It was nice, actually. I had dinner with Séb and Pauline. I love them. They asked about you. You should have come."

"I'm glad you've become friends."

"They want to set me up with some guy. A lawyer. Olivier."

"Olivier, the lawyer." I met her eyes and then looked away. I felt hollow and sick.

She sighed. "Anyway, I have class. I should get back."

"I'll take the trays in."

"Thanks." She stood up and touched my shoulder. "William," she said, and walked away toward the main building.

As I was returning from the cafeteria I saw Mazin reading on the grass in front of the upper school.

"What's up Maz?"

"Hey," he said and went back to his book.

"You doing O.K.?"

He nodded, keeping his eyes on the page.

"What's wrong, Maz?"

"Nothing." He shook his head. "Just work."

"Is there something bothering you?"

"Nope."

"O.K.," I said, looking down at him. But he ignored me and I left.

* * *

Later, when I returned to the English department Mia was sitting at her desk with Steven Connor.

"Hi guys."

"What up, Silver?"

Mia smiled at me.

"What'd you do this time?" I asked.

"Nothing, man. Have some faith. I'm trying to improve myself. Ms. Keller's almost as hard as you were."

I sat down at my desk. "Oh, I promise you she's much harder, Esteban. Much harder. She actually knows what she's talking about. She has lesson plans. I don't even read half the books I teach. Pay attention. This year you could actually learn something."

"O.K., O.K., Steven, back to work." She rolled her eyes at me and tapped the paper with her pen.

I pulled an essay from a pile and began to read.

"You need to focus your thesis, Steven. Make it more precise. 'Stephen Dedalus and Hamlet are similar for several reasons' is too vague."

"You think?" I said not looking up.

"Dude, you would have loved this essay."

"Not with *that* thesis, Esteban. Please."

"I don't understand."

"Ignore him. How can we focus this? Are you sure you believe it? *Are* they really similar?"

"Well, he makes a bunch of references to Hamlet in the book."

"The novel. O.K. Are you sure? And do those references immediately make the two characters similar? And what's another word for reference? Something a bit more literary?"

"What do you mean?"

"You know exactly what she means, Esteban." I turned in my chair and looked at him. "If you can't answer Ms. Keller's question I'm jumping out the window. And I have more willpower than that candy-ass Hamlet."

"He'll do it, Steven," Mia said, looking at me and laughing.

I opened the window.

Steven held his head in his hands. "References. References."

I pulled myself up and sat on the edge of the window frame. "I'm going. After all the work we did last year? *This* is how I'm repaid? With references? *References*, Esteban? Why don't you just spit in my face?"

"Allusions!" He yelled.

"Good," Mia said.

I dropped down to the floor and went back to my desk.

"Allusions, Mr. Silver, allusions!"

"Indeed, Steven. And thank you for saving Mr. Silver's life. Let's take a look at those allusions and try to develop a precise and focused thesis, O.K.? Maybe now, Mr. Silver will allow us to get some work done."

"I doubt it," Steven said laughing.

I went back to my essays but from time to time turned to watch them working together. Mia was so good with him, explaining the same ideas over and over again, keeping them new, approaching from different angles, never losing her patience, letting him make his arguments regardless of their quality.

"See here," Steven said, quoting Joyce, 'He came to the woman, the weaker vessel, and poured the poison of his eloquence into her ear.' It's just like what Claudius did to his brother."

"O.K., but is that enough?" She asked, looking at him seriously, giving him the time to work it out on his own.

"Put the novel down, Steven. Look at me. Forget about the essay."

Steven crossed his arms and looked up at her.

"Let's just have a conversation. Do you think that Dedalus and Hamlet are really similar characters?"

"I think so. I don't know."

"Of course you know. Stop being a student who has to write a paper for a moment. Just tell me what you think. Are they similar? I'd like to know what you think."

After a while he nodded his head. "Yes."

"O.K." Mia smiled at him. "Now tell me how."

I loved her there. Sitting in the office with the door closed, listening to Steven and Mia, I became sharply aware of how soon it would all be gone. I'd miss the shabby office, the coffee maker, my desk, the view from the window. I watched Mia leaning in, scribbling across his page, lost in teaching, and thought, Good-bye.

* * *

She said, "God, I hate those stairs."

Those stairs. As if they were ours. As if we should really do something about them, find another apartment, the two of us. She dropped into a chair and began pulling off her boots. Home after a long day. She stood up and kissed me on the mouth. "You've been drinking?" She walked to the fridge and, staring into the white light, looking for something to eat, she laughed and said, "And on a school night too."

Hours later, naked beneath one of my good shirts, her cheeks flushed, she stood by my window looking out across the city. I made us plates of pasta and put them on the table and called to her. She came and kissed me on the cheek. "This is perfect," she said. "This is exactly what I want to be doing. And then maybe I'll go down on you, for once." She grinned at me and raised her eyebrows. "You know I want to. It's just, the only time I've done it before. It was really horrible. Basically my ex-boyfriend, he sort of forced me to do it, you know. It was terrible. He had the back of my head and wouldn't let go."

She put a forkful of pasta into her mouth and chewed.

"Who was this?"

"Come on, Silver," she said, her mouth still full of spaghetti. "You don't want to know that."

"He goes to the school?"

"Yeah, he goes to the school. Can I have a glass of wine?"

I got up and opened a bottle.

"I'd like to kill him," I said touching her face.

She laughed and looked up at me, her eyes bright. "You're a sweet man," she said.

* * *

In the morning I could barely get out of bed. The apartment was very cold. I forced myself into the shower and stood beneath the steaming water until I was warm again. On the way to the *métro*, I passed a man slumped in a doorway and I nearly stopped. He looked dead. The streets were quiet. There were patches of ice in front of Bar du Marché. One of the morning waiters was scattering salt around his sidewalk.

Again the first one in the office, I opened the window to let the cold air fill the room. Again, the field was covered with a thin layer of frost the color of the sky. The poplar trees were bare.

I was still at the window when I heard a great grunt behind me and turned to find Mickey Gold settling into the deep couch, his legs spread out before him.

"Oh Christ, Will," he said clutching the inside of his right leg.

"Morning, Mickey," I said. I was happy to see him.

"Will, I tell you, I was watching the television last night and I sprained my groin. I've got these slippers with the no-slip grip, great things you know, cozy as hell, but they've got no slide. My grandkids gave them to me. They don't want me slipping down the stairs. I'm old as hell, Will, you know? So I sat down to watch the television and I spread my legs out like I am now and the goddamn slipper doesn't slip and bang, I've got a pain tearing up my leg like you can't imagine and now I can barely walk. What the hell? Pull your groin watching television? It's a wild world, Will. You can't possibly imagine. Pour me a cup of coffee? And close the damn window. I gotta keep my crotch warm."

I closed the window and poured him a cup of coffee.

For a moment he was unusually quiet.

"So, Will, I got to ask, what the hell's going on with you? You doing O.K.?"

"Yeah, Mickey, I'm fine."

"Well, you don't seem all that fine to me. You look like shit."

I shrugged.

"You look thin. Don't you eat? What do you do with yourself? You ever sleep?"

"It's been a tough year. I think maybe I'm just burned out. I've lost something. Can't quite seem to put it all in order."

He nodded, squinting at me, rubbing his groin. "Christ, this thing's killing me."

"I'm sorry about that."

"Forget it. That's the way it happens, Will. You're watching television, everything's great, and you pull your damn groin. There was a time if I pulled my groin I'd do it playing basketball. But that's just what happens."

I smiled at him.

"Mind if I give you some advice, Will?"

I shrugged. "Not at all. Could use some."

He looked at me for a long time. Then he shook his head as if answering the question before asking it. "You don't get much advice from people, do you? Your dad's not around? Mom?"

I shook my head. "No. Not anymore. Not for a couple of years."

"Both of them, gone?"

"Yeah," I said. "Both at once."

"At once?"

I nodded. "In an instant," I said.

Slowly he drew his legs up and leaned forward, his elbows on his knees. He grimaced in pain and made a slight grunt. "You were close?"

I nodded and felt that familiar cold stillness.

"Christ," he whispered. "Brothers or sisters?"

"No."

He took a deep breath and blew it out hard. "Ah, Will. That's a hard thing." He shook his head and looked down at his hands. "Never married?" He asked, his voice softer now.

"I was."

"What happened? I mean if you don't mind me asking you."

"I left. When my parents died. I left. I came here."

He seemed so sad slumped down on that couch looking at me.

After a while, I said, "You were going to give me some advice."

He shrugged his shoulders. "Will, you ask me, you're falling apart. I'm sorry but you look like a raccoon with those circles under your eyes. You don't talk to anybody, you walk around here like a zombie. I'm gonna tell you, that's more than frustration, buddy. That's more than 'I'm sick of being a teacher, the magic's gone,' that's something else. Will, listen, don't waste your time thinking you can do the whole thing alone. No matter what kind of shit you've lived through. And I can only imagine, though I've had my share. Don't go it alone. Buddy, it's a recipe for misery, you hear me? You're what? Twenty-seven? Twenty-eight?"

"Thirty-three."

"Then be happy you look as young as you do. I was your age I'd lost half my hair. Will, it's disappointment from here on in, you understand me? There's nothing interesting about you anymore. You see what I mean? You're gonna start to bore the hell out of yourself. You're out of surprises, you've squeezed what you can out of yourself. The world disappoints you, Will. Nearly always, the world disappoints you. You know that by now, don't you," he said nodding his head.

He took another gulp of coffee.

"Look, I don't know what's going on in your life, what you do all goddamn day, but I know this: You can't do it alone. You're young. You think you're strong as hell. You think you can think it all out? Stare out your window and the answers come?" He shook his head. "The answers don't come. And you know why?"

"Because there are no answers?"

"There *are* answers Will. And you can save your sarcasm for someone not as smart as I am. Figure it out, Will. You can't do it alone. You understand me? Of course you do. I'd bet anything you've got yourself all tangled up with some gorgeous nightmare of a girl. I'll put next month's paycheck on it. You want in? Some girl you barely speak to? Who follows you around like a golden retriever?"

I laughed and shook my head.

"Will, listen to me. If you don't remember anything else, remember this: Anyone you can fool isn't worth loving. You understand me? It's a young man's move. You're young but, buddy, you're not *that* young. It's a coward's game, you understand? Teachers. We live for too long on those adoring eyes and then one day, it's just not enough. It's nothing at all but if you're not careful, it'll be all you have. You understand me? I know, I know, I sound like a song, but you understand what I'm saying?"

I nodded.

"I'm not telling you to go get married. Marriage won't save you. Find some friends. Find some people you give a shit about. Who care about you. Who are *smarter* than you are. Find a woman, Will. Who laughs at you. Who'll kick your ass out of the house. You find that woman and she's the same woman who'll throw herself in front of a truck for you? Well, then you're somewhere. You're a great teacher, Will. No question. Born natural. Good-looking too. Passionate as hell. Heart too big for your own good. You've got the world. For fuck's sake, what else do you want?"

He struggled out of the couch, groaning the whole time. When he'd finally pulled himself up he walked over and put his heavy hand on my shoulder and looked down at me.

"What was her name?"

"Isabelle."

"You ever think about going back?"

I didn't say anything.

"I don't know, Will. Maybe there's a chance. Maybe she's still around. Cowards spend their lives alone. Either with people who can't hurt them, or with no one at all. Either way, man. Same thing."

He squeezed my shoulder. "You be tougher than that, Will. You do the hard thing."

He smiled.

"I got to get out of here, buddy. Take care of yourself."

"You too, Mickey."

I could still feel the weight of his hand, the heat of it on my shoulder as I listened to his footsteps fading down the long hallway toward his classroom.

* * *

After he was gone, I gathered my things and left the office before anyone else arrived. I went to my classroom and prepared to spend the morning teaching three sections of sophomore English.

I placed copies of the second chapter of *Walden* on the empty desks fanned in a semi-circle before the whiteboard. Then I wrote the day's quotation across the board:

"If we are really dying, let us hear the rattle in our throats and feel cold in the extremities. If we are alive, let us go about our business."

Each of my sophomores had a separate notebook in which they'd write a ten-minute response to the day's quotation. Those ten minutes were often my favorite part of the day, sitting on the edge of my desk, drinking coffee, watching them write, smiling at the students who looked up at me. I loved the ones who chewed on their pen caps and furrowed their brows, pretending to think hard. I loved watching the few kids who got lost in their work. The sound of the room, the pens across paper, the exaggerated sighs of exasperation.

I used to think, These are my students. I love them. I was often amazed by the closeness I felt, by my desire to protect them, to push them. I wanted to make them proud of me. I wanted never to disappoint them. As much as I loved them in those quiet minutes at the beginning of class, I also wanted them to love me in return.

After I'd written the quotation across the board, I sat at one of their desks and looked up at the board. I watched myself, book in hand, pacing, asking questions. Teaching.

There was noise in the halls—laughing, lockers slamming, familiar voices.

The ten-minute bell rang. I looked down at the packet and read:

Let us settle ourselves, and work and wedge our feet downward through the mud and slush of opinion, and prejudice, and tradition, and delusion, and appearance, that alluvion which covers the globe, through Paris and London, through New York and Boston and Concord, through Church and State, through poetry and philosophy and religion, till we come to a hard bottom and rocks in place, which we can call reality, and say, This is, and no mistake; and then begin, having a *point d'appui* . . . Be it life or death, we crave only reality. If we are really dying, let us hear the rattle in our throats and feel cold in the extremities; if we are alive, let us go about our business . . . The intellect is a cleaver; it discerns and rifts its way into the secret of things . . . My head is hands and feet . . . my head is an organ for burrowing . . . I think that the richest vein is somewhere hereabouts; so by the divining-rod and thin rising vapors I judge; and here I will begin to mine.

From Thoreau's *Walden,* Chapter 2, "Where I Lived, and What I Lived For."

After the bell rang, after they'd written their ten-minute

responses, we began. What did he mean? I asked again and again. What did he mean by "and here I will begin to mine?" And how is the "intellect a cleaver?" And is it really? And are we really mining? And should we be? And do we "only crave reality?" And should we? And what about morality? And is there such a thing? And what are these "thin rising vapors?" And are your heads "hands and feet?" Are your heads organs "for burrowing?" And if so, what hills are yours burrowing through? And what have you found so far?

* * *

When the bell rang that last period before lunch, I was exhausted. I'd been caught up in those rotating discussions, every hour beginning again. When the last class filtered out I stood alone at my desk, collecting papers, slowly stacking extra handouts.

There was a moment then when it was as if my exhaustion were only physical. I took a deep breath and walked out into the hall, down the stairs, and along the field toward the cafeteria.

I saw in the eyes of those people passing that there were things happening around me, things beyond my control, and I was tumbling forward.

I bought a sandwich and smiled at Jean-Paul, who waved at me from the back of the kitchen. I felt a sudden tenderness for him. I wanted to put an arm around his shoulder. But I knew it was only nostalgia for my first days in Paris when Jean-Paul and his terrible food were novel pleasures.

The morning fog had burned off and the high clouds were gone, there was bright sunlight on the field. I stood at the far side, where the bare poplars lined the fence. From there I could look back at the school. Sitting on the grass, still damp from the morning's dew and fog, I felt the cold moisture soaking through my jeans.

I ate and watched faculty and students come outside. The younger kids ran screaming out of the buildings, girls clutching each other.

Now there were kids everywhere, chasing, reading in the sun, studying for exams, all of us dreading the bell sure to ring.

I looked out at the picnic benches, and the stream of students flowing between the school and the cafeteria. And then I closed my eyes.

Soon, I felt someone touch a warm hand against the back of my neck.

Mia said, "I'll see you at lit mag and if you want to have a beer tonight. Or whenever, I'm around."

"Thanks," I said, keeping my eyes closed. "I'd love to. We'll do it."

After a moment I opened my eyes and squinting into the sun, I watched her walk away.

The bell rang and the field emptied, the students funneled dutifully back inside as if drawn by some great magnet and I stayed there as long as I could, until my next class began fifty minutes later.

MARIE

I don't know what happened to make him change his mind for the second time. But one day he said yes. I mean just like that. And that's when it really started. The two of us. I mean we were a couple in our way. Lovers anyway. Real lovers.

I came after school. On the weekends. Whenever he let me, I'd come. I'd sit clutching my phone like an idiot, waiting for him to send his permission. I hated him for that but by then I was his. Long before then really. Like I said, I'd have done anything he asked.

We had a routine. I'd walk up those fucking stairs. We'd lock the door. Sometimes it was gentle. Other times it was rough. I guess like any other couple. And that's the thing really. For a while, it felt as if we were just like any other couple. Sometimes I'd bring bread, or a bottle of wine. I liked the idea of shopping for him. I used to pretend that it was our apartment, that we lived together, like it was our normal life. It was easy to do that. For a while it was easy, anyway. We'd make love or fuck or whatever we were doing, and eventually I started to have orgasms with him. He was very patient. He was always whispering in my ear. He hypnotized me that way. He was always encouraging me to tell him what I liked. This? This? Like this?

You have to talk to me, Marie, he'd say. Just let yourself go. Tell me what you want, he'd say, like I had any fucking idea what I wanted. But, still, I felt like a queen the way he treated me in bed. He was so delicate, so precise, so, and this sounds strange but it's right—he was elegant. He gave me so much attention and eventually I just gave in, just came unlocked, you know? I was loud and wild and happy.

Afterward, with my face all flushed, he'd tell me how beautiful I was. And I loved it. I did. Really. But I started to have the impression that I was making love to a ghost or a phantom or something. And more than once I felt that I could have been anyone. Anyone at all. As if what he was doing with me there in that apartment wasn't much different from what he did at school, what he did in the classroom.

I don't know. I'm not sure I really actually thought those things at the time. It was more a feeling, a sort of dark hum I didn't want to listen to. But I do remember that feeling, that sense that he wasn't really there, that he was just doing a job. I don't know, it's a strange thing to say, and yet it seems exactly right.

The best days were when there was nowhere to go, when I didn't need to get home. When it was like that I was happier than I'd ever been in my life. He'd cook for me or play me music or we'd watch a film. Whatever it was, there was always a lesson. How to make a sauce, or why some musician mattered, that kind of thing. You can say what you want but then, at the time, it was a dream. I'd come from ISF and walk through the city all gray and cold and mean and enter that code, a number I kept thinking of as secret and magical. He took me in and fed me and made love to me. I mean through that door and up those stairs it was a warm, beautiful world. I didn't want anything else. How anyone couldn't understand that was beyond me.

I started to sleep there. I'd go over on Saturday night after being out with Ariel. At first I'd leave him at three or four in the morning. He asked me to stay but I couldn't figure out how to organize all the lies. But finally I just said O.K. And when he asked me, I told him my parents thought I was sleeping at

Ariel's. And where does Ariel think you're sleeping? At home, I said. And that was that. The problem, the real problem, was Ariel. Once I stopped sleeping at her apartment she just lost her mind. At a certain point I stopped going there at all. I left some things at his place and would spend Saturday night and all of Sunday and then I'd take the RER home in the early evening.

I'd sit on the train with that late-Sunday dread, that heavy winter sadness made worse because I was racing away from him, going exactly in the wrong direction. After that, after I cut her out, Ariel barely spoke to me. Or we barely spoke to each other. That kind of thing happened all the time. We were inseparable and then it was over. Girls changed friends all year long. You were part of someone's life. Knew their parents. And then you'd never see each other again. In that way we were prepared.

I didn't care about anything else. My entire life for a while. I mean there was nothing else. Nothing. And one day I told him. We were in bed and I looked at him and I said it. Will, I love you, I said and he looked like I'd told him the sky was blue. We made love afterward and maybe he was sweet to me but all I could think about was that expression and how he lay there not moving looking like he was dead.

At school I started sitting outside his classroom. There was this space between where the lockers ended and his door, maybe three feet of empty wall. I used to sit there and pretend to study. I was like a dog or something, sitting outside his door. These are the things you do. I'd sit and listen. I'd stare into my book, sitting on the cold polished floor, in that awful gray hallway with my head resting against the wall, trying to hear everything, to be with him, not to miss a moment.

Those kids adored him. Unless you listened to him teach, saw him, you can't understand. I loved listening to his voice, thinking about the things he was saying.

One day I heard him make a comment in class and it sounded so familiar to me and I realized that I'd already heard it, that he'd said it a few days before. I don't remember exactly what it was, just that he'd said it to me. We were lying in bed and it was the same sentence, the same cadence, the same inflection.

It was awful and suddenly I had that same terrible feeling, as if he was a ghost, or I was a ghost, and that he'd never love me. I was just filling space.

GILAD

He'd never been so late. Twenty minutes had passed and nothing. I thought of him waiting at Odéon the day we saw Christophe Jolivet die. I looked around at my classmates and imagined their lives to come. It seemed to me that without Silver we were all doomed somehow. Rick sat with his arms folded across his chest looking at the closed door. There was something wistful in his expression and I watched his eyes until he glanced at me. He nodded, almost indiscernibly. Hala looked away from the room out to the poplars. Lily smiled sadly at me. Abdul rocked back and forth, from time to time quickly running his thin fingers through his curly hair. What would he become, this nervous kid so paralyzed? In black ink, Cara drew an intricate design across a white page. Aldo slept on his desk, his hair across his face. Jane straightened the books on her desk and then she opened her notebook. On a blank page she wrote, "December 13, 2002." I watched her hand, the black nail polish replaced by a clear varnish, move slowly over the page: December 13, 2002, retracing the date again and again, December 13, 2002, December 13, 2002, December 13, 2002. The tip of her pen followed the deepening line, the pressure forming a groove in the soft paper.

"He's probably not coming," Hala said.

I glanced up at her surprised.

Rick looked at Hala and nodded knowingly.

Cara shook her head. "Unbelievable," she said.

"What?" I said.

No one answered.

Colin was staring at me with a strange expression on his face. When our eyes met it seemed as if he were apologizing for something.

We were so quiet waiting there. So still. And I thought: This is exactly where we are. Friday morning. December 13. 2002. This is exactly where we are, waiting for the next thing. December 13, 2002. I concentrated on the fake wood grain of my desk.

In the stillness of the morning, I felt such affection for all of us in that single moment of our lives. Everything was tenuous. Everything was fragile. The flat gray light outside, the black leafless poplars, the frost on the field, the muffled voices filtering through the thin walls. This is where we are. December 13, 2002.

* * *

When the door opened and we saw that it was him, what we felt, I promise you, what we *all* felt, was relief. He carried with him a stack of novels.

"Bad morning," he said. "Sorry I'm late. *As I Lay Dying.* William Faulkner," he said, handing out the books.

"We haven't even talked about *l'Etranger,*" Hala grumbled.

"No, Hala, you're right we haven't. And we will, but I'd like you to have this and begin reading it. You'll be able to move through it slowly. It'll be an opportunity, a chance to savor a novel rather than read it under duress."

He smiled. But Aldo, who'd been sitting glumly with his chin on his desk, laughed smugly. "Savor it?"

"Indeed Aldo, savor. Like a piece of pie."

"Whatever."

Silver turned, looking at him for the first time.

"Aldo," he said sternly as if beginning a speech. And again in mock sadness, shaking his head, "Aldo."

He turned to us and began.

"Every text is understood by each of us differently. We cannot separate our experience from the way that we read. Our experience informs our reading in the same way that it informs our lives, what we see on the street, how we interact with people, and so on. Which is why you might argue that there's no single truth, no absolutely common experience. Both *l'Etranger* and *As I Lay Dying* deal, in their own ways, with this same idea. As you read, you'll see that Faulkner and Camus have more in common than you might first imagine." He looked around the room. And then he said what he always did, "What am I talking about?"

He folded his arms across his chest and waited. I watched him up there, that familiar expression, the cocky demeanor, the posture of expectation, of control. He'd been charming, had spoken with those irregular pauses, a slight grin when he'd suggested the possibility of savoring the novel. And again the restrained smile, amused with himself.

I raised my hand.

He faced me and gave a slight bow. "Gilad," he said, "Tell us."

"I think the point is, well, I think that's right. Everything we've experienced determines how we experience other experiences. Something like that. Each person sees the world slightly differently. So, the same should be true with something we read. I guess because reading is another experience."

He nodded and he had the look on his face that always made me proud.

"Obviously," Hala said, "there are many people who believe in a single truth, Mr. Silver. But it's obvious to me that, I mean, it is an impossible, stupid, childish idea. I read a book, or see a film, or even go to a party, what I see there, what I take away from those experiences can never be the same as what someone else takes away."

"Yes, Hala," he encouraged. "And let me make clear that these are not my ideas; I certainly wasn't the one to come up with them. These are the principles of deconstruction, the notion, essentially, that the reader, as much as, if not more than, the author provides meaning to a text. We, as readers, apply our experience, our knowledge, not to mention our ignorance, to the meaning of a given work. This is interesting as literary theory, but for our purposes, I think more interesting if we apply it to our lives, to the way we view not only texts, but also the world around us. Does everyone see what I mean?"

Cara didn't understand. How could a paragraph not mean precisely the same thing to every reader?

Silver wrote a sentence across the board: "The dog ran across the field."

"Consider this sentence. Read it to yourselves a few times." He waited and then read aloud, "The dog ran across the field. The dog ran across the field. Rick, what does the sentence mean?"

"A dog ran across a field?" He looked flatly back at Silver.

"Yes, O.K., fine. But give me your interpretation of the sentence."

"There's nothing to interpret, a dog ran across a field."

"I agree," Abdul said, eyes on his desk. "It's obvious."

"No mate, what *you* see is obvious, but the sentence might mean different things to other people," Colin said.

Silver nodded and folded his arms. He turned to Lily, twirling a braid in her fingers, studying the board. He kept his eyes on her.

"What do you see Lily? I mean exactly."

She shrugged. "Ummm, there's a little white dog, he's missing a leg, and he runs with this weird limp. He's small and the field is all covered with snow and he leaves his little tracks as he goes."

She never took her eyes off the board, and when she finished we all laughed. She shrugged her shoulders again and said, "That's the dog I see."

Which was precisely what Silver wanted. And he knew Lily would give an answer like that. Then the bell rang and we were left with an image of a three-legged dog limping across a field of snow.

Winter break began the next day.

WILL

N othing was the same.
We'd never see each other outside of the apartment.
She'd come over and lock the door. We watched movies
together. She complained about her parents.

"You'll survive it all," I told her.

All month it was cold and gray outside. She walked around
the apartment naked. She called me an old man. One Sunday
morning we woke up and she said, "I love you."

She shook her head. "I know you don't love me. But I love
you. Will you fuck me like you love me?"

I didn't say anything. I was as gentle and kind as I knew how
to be. I touched her as softly as I could. I kissed her slowly.

"Make love to me," she said. And I did. As best I could.

After she came, she cried and I held onto her. She pressed
her head against my chest. I kissed her hair. "It's O.K.," I said.
"It'll be O.K."

"I love you, Will. William." It was the first time she'd called
me by my first name.

We lay there for a while in silence. "I'm going to get us
breakfast Marie. Stay here. I'll be back."

I climbed out of bed, got dressed and stood in line at
Carton. As I was leaving the bakery, Julia Tompkins and her
mother walked in.

"Oh my God, Mr. Silver!"

She hugged me. Mrs. Tompkins smiled. "Having a nice
Sunday, Mr. Silver?"

I imagined Marie asleep in my bed.

"I can't believe you live around here." Julia laughed. "We live like five seconds away. We come here all the time. They make the best bread in the world. We're totally neighbors."

Mrs. Tompkins shook her head at her daughter's enthusiasm. "Julia's a big fan. I'm sure you know that by now."

"Shut *up*, Mom."

"Both Rick and Julia are big fans."

I forced a laugh.

"I should get back," I said holding up my bag of croissants.

"Have a great rest of the weekend," Mrs. Tompkins said.

"See you on Monday, Mr. Silver."

When I arrived home, Marie was standing at the sink, washing dishes.

"Hi honey," she said. "How was work?"

I spooned coffee into the old Bialetti and she wrapped her arms around me.

We drank our coffee and ate the croissants with raspberry jam. They were playing an old Sidney Bechet concert on TSF. It had begun to rain.

"Will, I'm so happy," she said. "I've never been so happy. Never."

I smiled at her. Her cheeks were flushed, her hair a mess. She was naked beneath one of my old shirts. She looked prettier than I'd ever seen her.

We lay in bed listening to the rain, the street noise outside. Marie told me how she wasn't afraid of anything. How powerful she'd begun to feel, how confident.

"You see the way I walk around your apartment, Will? Like nothing can go wrong. Like I'm the queen of the world, the smartest, toughest, most beautiful woman in the universe? I'm going to feel that way in the street someday."

I smiled at the ceiling.

"Laugh all you want, asshole. You'll see." She sat up and looked at me. "You know what I'm going to do? One day?"

I shook my head. It was hard to resist her when she was like this.

"You want to know what I'm going to do when you're old, I mean even older than you are now? When I'm even *more* beautiful and you can barely get up those fucking stairs?"

I laughed. "Tell me."

"I'm going to have my own school. Outside Paris. Like in Saint-Denis for poor kids who are getting fucked by France and it'll be full of teachers like Ms. Keller and you."

I watched her and listened. Her eyes so full of light.

"You think now just because I'm who I am at ISF, I won't be someone else later? You think that, don't you?"

"I like who you are now, Marie. More and more to tell you the truth. And I know you're right. I know you'll do all of it. Everything you want to do. I just have to look at you to know."

"Queen of the fucking world, Will. You'll see."

"I believe you, Marie."

She lay back down, resting her head on my chest. "You'll see. A beautiful school. And out there, I'll feel every day like I feel in here."

I held her tight against me.

"Are you happy?" she asked.

I looked at her, touched her face, and said, yes.

It was true.

* * *

For a while there were days like these. Afternoons after school watching movies, making love in a chair by the window, lying in bed awake together in the early evening, watching the room darken.

Marie came after school and late on Saturday nights when she'd arrive long after I'd gone to sleep, bringing the smell of evening with her. She'd slide beneath the blankets, waking me with her cool body. We'd tear at each other and, particularly when she was drunk, she'd push herself against me desperately. And on those gray Sunday mornings, I'd play music she'd never heard—Keith Jarrett, Dinah Washington. It was always cold outside and there was never any sunshine—only the dull Paris grisaille and often, the steady rain falling against the roof like gravel against a drum.

Once, I was waiting for the doors of the train to close when Mia and Marie walked into the car. The three of us sat together—Mia at my side, Marie facing us.

"So what are you doing on this train?" Mia asked.

"Shopping with Ariel, hot chocolate at the Flore," she answered, looking Mia in the eyes.

So she can lie, I thought.

* * *

Days later, I had lunch with Mia at La Palette.

"You seem better," she told me.

"I am," I said.

"I'm glad." She looked at me briefly and then cast her eyes away. "You can tell me anything, you know."

I nodded. "I know, Mia."

"Are there a lot of things you don't tell me?"

"I guess there are a lot of things I don't tell anyone. Like most people."

She touched my hand. "You'll be all right, Will."

"How are things with Olivier, the lawyer?"

She shrugged.

The café was filling with people. Charlie Parker came on playing "Lover Man" and the dark-haired woman reading the paper behind the bar turned it up loud. We listened to the music, looking at each other, our empty plates in front of us.

"You could come home with me, you know. Spend Christmas with my lunatic family."

"Mia," I said.

"You could come, Will. I don't know, we could . . . " she trailed off.

The next day she left for Chicago and I stayed in Paris.

* * *

A few days before she left to go skiing with her family, Marie came over and wouldn't sit down. She paced frantically around the apartment. She pushed me onto the floor and rode me angrily. She looked down at me, her eyes narrowed. I never saw her blink.

"Hold my hair," she said. "Pull it."

Afterward there was blood on her knees.

We lay together until we got cold. She stood up and wrapped a blanket around her body.

"Ariel thinks you're so hot," she said.

"I doubt that."

"Don't. She told me. She says it all the time."

"She's pretty horrible to me in class, Marie. I doubt—"

"Probably because you're sleeping with me and not her, Will."

I sat up. "Marie, have you told her?"

"Jesus. No. It was a joke, a fucking joke. *Putain!* Calm down.

She hates her dad. That's why she's always so pissy. It's nothing to do with you, Will. Believe me, she'd fuck you in a second. She told me yesterday."

"Yesterday?"

"On the phone."

"How'd that come up?" I watched her biting her nail.

"She brought you up, I guess. She wants you. What's the big deal?" She glanced up and looked at me, "Does that excite you Will? Would you like to fuck Ariel?" She stared at me.

"No, Marie."

She was walking around the apartment, picking things up, pretending to look at books on the shelves.

She went to the window and looked out at the city. I watched her standing naked, the curtains falling around her. Then she turned. She was shivering.

"Once, her father tried to seduce me." She crossed her arms across her chest.

I didn't say anything, just pulled the blanket around my knees.

"I was in Ariel's bedroom waiting for her to come home from a run. I was sitting on her bed. He came in and tried to seduce me."

I nodded, watching her.

"But then Ariel came home and caught us. Well, caught him."

"Doing what?"

"Nothing. He was just sitting on the bed with me. He said he'd help me with my homework. He had his hand on my leg when Ariel came in. That's it, O.K.? But she was so mad. She didn't talk to me for like two weeks."

She sat down on the floor next to me. I pulled the blanket around us and stroked her back with my hand.

"But that was all? Nothing more? Just his hand on your leg?"

"Nothing more, Will."

"Does Ariel know, Marie? I mean about us. Have you told anyone?"

She looked at me briefly and then turned to the window where the light was flat and weak.

"Just tell me, Marie. I need to know." I took a slow breath. "Please, Marie tell me if—"

"No," she whispered pulling away. "No one knows. I haven't told anyone. O.K.?"

"O.K.," I said. "O.K." I pulled her against me.

"I'd never tell anyone, Will," she said beginning to cry. "Never. I know what it would do. To you. To us. Why would I? Fuck, Will why would I?"

"It's all right. Forget it."

She was sobbing, her body shuddering. I held her and I knew.

Soon, Marie went home and I stayed on the floor.

* * *

Those weeks I sat in cafés reading. I went to the movies. At night I went to La Palette and drank. I slept late, often until the afternoon. I missed Marie and as the city emptied, the streets quieter and quieter the closer we came to Christmas, the more I wished she'd return.

She wrote messages to me. I love you, Will. I miss you, Will. God, I miss your body. *Comme tu me manques!*

I picked at a roasted chicken on Christmas day and drank a bottle of Bordeaux.

When they were alive, I'd sit with my parents around the tree and we'd open presents. On Christmas Eve, a few months before they died, we drove up to spend a week with them. The four of us had dinner while it snowed hard outside.

My parents. Me and Isabelle.

My dad built a fire after dinner and we all sat in the living room eating pecan pie. Afterward, Isabelle lay on the couch with her head in my lap. The four of us stayed up for hours watching the snow fall out of darkness through pale porch light.

Now I sat at the small table in my apartment. There was the hum of the room. The sound of the blade cutting through the chicken. The sound of wine in my throat. Returning the glass to the table. I tried to be perfectly still. I held my breath and imagined myself alone in Paris. In a room in a city holding my breath.

* * *

A few days after Christmas she sent me a message.

I was alone in a café reading *Hopscotch*.

I'm pregnant.

MARIE

We went to Megève for Christmas. The whole family thing. My sister was there. The four of us. My parents had rented a chalet for the break. It was cozy with a wide stone fireplace and everyone was happy. I loved being with my dad who'd promised to stay the entire time. Sometimes we skied together, just the two of us. He was very sweet. He drank less than usual. He asked about school and I remember wishing I could tell him everything about my secret life. We'd sit on the lift together, warm in the sun, all wrapped up in our parkas, and talk and talk. He made me laugh. He told me stories about China, where he'd been spending most of his time. He'd been gone so often I'd forgotten how much I adored him and I kept wanting to tell him the truth. Somehow I don't think he would have been angry. He would never have made a scene, or gone to the school or anything like that.

It doesn't matter. In the end I never told him.

* * *

I was late.

I stayed home that day and while everyone else was skiing I went to the little pharmacy on the square by the church and bought a pregnancy test.

I took it home and sat in the bathroom and when I saw it

was positive I went numb. After a while I sent him a message. I can't imagine what it did to him. All I wrote was, I'm pregnant. That's it. I mean after all the messages I'd been sending— I miss you, I miss you. And then this. But it was what I could manage. Maybe I wanted to punish him, I don't know. I didn't say a thing to anyone. I kept it to myself until one night I didn't think I'd survive. I got out of bed and snuck out of the house. It was late. Cold. The streets were covered with fresh snow and there was that round silence that comes in the winter at night in the mountains. I walked and walked and then I called him. He sounded so far away. But he was nice to me.

You couldn't have asked for more. He said he'd be there. We'd get through it together. We'd do whatever I wanted. I needed to think about it. To really think about it. I told him I didn't want to think about it. I told him I wanted *him* to tell me what to do and he said he couldn't do that. He said it wasn't his choice, that it was my body, and all that. I was standing in the snow crying, feeling the way I'd felt on the bridge the night I'd called Ariel a bitch. He said, Try to sleep, Marie. I'm here for you. I'm right here, he said, in the saddest voice I'd ever heard.

The next night I called back and told him I didn't know what to do and then he said that he didn't think it was a good idea to have the baby. Something like that. He kept saying, But Marie I don't want to push you to do anything you don't want to do. He said over and over again, I'll be there no matter what. I mean, he was perfect. His words were perfect. But it was also as if he was reading a script. Part of me just wanted him to say, Get a fucking abortion goddamn it. You know, to prove that he cared at all. I mean about anything. But all he said was, I'm here, Marie. I'll be there the whole time. No matter what happens. Which is what you *want* someone to say to you. Still, I couldn't shake the feeling, that same feeling that I'd had from the beginning, that he was only a ghost, vacant, repeating lines.

For the rest of the time we were in Megève I tried to pretend it wasn't there. And I could do it during the day. I skied hard and stayed as close to my dad as I could. Sometimes on the lift, when it was just the two of us, I'd lean my head against his shoulder while he looked at the map and I'd cry beneath my goggles.

Then at night I'd lie in bed and try to imagine a child inside me, what it would look like, how it would resemble him, you know? Slowly I began to love it. Slowly it took on a personality. It had a face. I began to see it as a boy and then I imagined him with eyes just like his. Despite all the panic and dread of those last few days in the mountains, I was able to find a sort of center of warmth in this fantasy that I would give birth and the three of us would live together in his apartment in Paris. It's what kept me alive.

* * *

He insisted I see a doctor as if there might be a doubt. I knew. I was pregnant. There wasn't a question. But in Paris I went, for him. The day we got back I told my parents I was going to see Ariel and I went straight to the clinic. I waited there alone for hours. I was in a trance. I sat staring at the wall numb and frightened. He wanted to come but I told him not to. I think I was afraid he'd be angry, that he'd hate me for being pregnant.

By the time it was over it was nearly dark, and I had to go home. They did the tests and handed me the papers and I took them to school, which was the first place I saw him after break. It was terrible. We walked around and around the field with kids whispering and looking at us and me handing him the papers like we were doing some illegal business deal. I couldn't even touch him. I couldn't even look at him really. It was cruel and it was brutal. Walking there together, this baby inside me, his baby, and I couldn't even touch him. My God, you should have seen his face.

That afternoon I took the train straight to his apartment where we got into bed and I cried and cried. Then I sat up and looked at him. I'd never felt so hopeful in my entire life. It only lasted a moment. I was so happy for those few seconds, a sort of short burst of hope, of joy. As if we'd be O.K., the two of us. Together. Me and him.

WILL

I came back to school and met Marie at lunch. She handed me an envelope. "In case you don't believe me," she said. We walked long, slow circles around the field.

"Of course I believe you, Marie. Whatever you want to do. Whatever you decide. I'm here. No matter what," I told her looking at the thin piece of paper.

"I want to get an abortion," she said quietly. "I'm sorry for all of this. But you know, we're going to be fine. We'll be great, the two of us. One day we will."

She stopped walking and turned to me and forced a smile. "*Us*. I'm not stupid. No, listen to me. No matter what happens, Will. All of this? Nothing. It's. It'll be nothing. You're going to be great no matter what. You'll see. Trust me. I'm young, but I know some things."

She moved her hand as if to touch my face, caught herself, and started walking again. She whispered, "My God, you look sad."

We walked in silence for a while.

And then I said, "Just think about it, Marie. For you. Whatever you want to do. I'll support anything you decide. And when you're sure, tell me."

"Hey," she said. "You don't have to be any better than you are, O.K.? And I'm sure."

* * *

One of those days, Lily's white dog, missing a leg, limped across a field covered with snow. The bell rang and they left with their clean copies of *As I Lay Dying*.

* * *

It was very early. I'd forgotten to leave the heater on and from beneath the blankets I could see my breath in the morning air. I forced myself out of bed, took a shower and got dressed. The moon was a fang in the lightening sky.

I stood close to the heater but couldn't stop shivering.

I locked the door behind me and put my coat on in the staircase.

I turned up my collar but it did no good. I walked faster. There were street cleaners moving along the rue de Seine spraying away the night's garbage, avoiding two neighborhood drunks lying unconscious together on the sidewalk. The guy working the hose turned it off and signaled for the truck to stop. He kneeled down and shook the one who wasn't wearing shoes.

"*Il est vivant ou quoi?*" The driver asked leaning his head out, laughing.

The heaters were out on the train and I pulled my coat tighter. I was grateful for the cold. It gave me something to focus on. It kept me awake. I watched as we passed through station after station, the blank-faced commuters waiting in the dark for their trains. No one spoke. There was only the sound of the rattling car.

I was early and found a café by the RER station. I stood at the bar and drank a coffee, but couldn't face eating anything. The man standing next to me was smoking with a trembling hand. There was a beer on the bar in front of him. For a moment

I thought I might order one too. It had been a long time since I'd had a drink so early in the morning. I knew Marie would've been disappointed to smell alcohol on my breath. I ordered another coffee and waited.

When it was time, I paid the barman, walked up the street, and found her waiting by the taxi stand. When she saw me she pushed herself off the wall. We stood looking at each other, the street between us, waiting for the light to change, cars speeding by. I crossed and held her to me, my lips against her hair. It was the first time we'd touched in a public place.

In the taxi she gave the driver the address. We sat holding hands. Marie looked out her window and I looked out mine.

At the hospital, I paid the driver. The streetlights flickered off as the taxi drove away.

Not speaking, we walked along the straight stone hallways. The sound of our footsteps echoed off the stone walls and the vaulted cathedral ceilings. In the clinic there were green plastic chairs and Formica tables. There were polished floors and a nurses' station encased in glass.

They took us after an hour and put us in a room with another couple. The woman was on her side, her back to us, arms around her belly, in a black recliner in the corner. The man sat next to her and nodded at me. The nurse touched the woman's arm.

Marie and I sat at a table in the center of the room. "O.K.," she said squeezing my hand. "It's going to be fine, you'll see."

The nurse brought a small cup with the pills inside. Marie took them with water and went to the bathroom to change her clothes.

When she came back she wore a hooded IFS sweatshirt and baggy sweatpants "to hide the diaper," she said rolling her eyes.

We sat together reading magazines and waited and when we heard crying we locked eyes and didn't look away. Marie leaned forward and whispered to me across the table, "It won't be like that for me."

"It's O.K. if it is," I said.

"But it won't be," she promised, squeezing my hand, looking directly into my eyes. She was so sure of herself. She put her magazine away and began to read her copy of *The Waves*, underlining for Mia as she went.

They brought her some food but she refused to eat. I ate the crackers.

I watched her try to read and imagined a different life, where at the end of the day we'd have a child rather than be rid of one. Where I'd come home joyful instead of unburdened.

From time to time Marie would look up at me from her homework and smile. I imagined her sitting at our kitchen table, our baby asleep in the other room.

When the pain began she clenched her jaw. I touched her hand. She looked at me and I felt, again, what it was to be loved like that, and not to love in return. Soon she let go of my hand, stood up and walked awkwardly to the bathroom.

I watched the door close behind her. I heard the bolt slide into place.

I sat at the table beneath the fluorescent light and listened to it hum. Then I heard the toilet flush, the deep groaning of liquid being sucked down into the bowels of the building.

When she came out she was dressed in her street clothes. She had her bag over her shoulder. None of it was invention or artifice. Whatever lies she'd told me made no difference. As I watched her walk toward me I wanted to protect her. Whatever pain she'd endured she'd looked at me steadily, barely winced, and refused any weakness.

"That's it," she said. "You call the nurse."

They took Marie's temperature. Listened to her heart.

Then we were back in the long stone hallways trying to find our way out.

Just before walking into the day, we sat together on a low bench. I kissed her forehead.

"I'm happy," she said, looking at me with her flashing eyes.

We took separate taxis back to school, where she returned to class and I returned to work.

MARIE

He looked terrible—pale and exhausted with such dark circles under his eyes. God he was thin. He crossed the street and kissed me and held me tightly. It was the first time we'd touched out in the open. We were in front of the station with all the taxis in a row, their lights on.

Then we were in the back and the taxi was moving. He didn't say anything so I told the driver where to go. I thought, I've never really heard him speak French. And then I felt as if I might take care of him. I tried to imagine what it would be like to introduce him to my parents.

When we stopped in front of the hospital there was a part of me that was happy to be there. Maybe that's disgusting. The idea that I'd have been happy, that anything that morning would have brought me pleasure. But it wouldn't be true to say otherwise. Amid the fear, the nausea, I was there with him. Just the two of us. We sat in that dreary waiting room holding hands. There were other couples there, people around, but he still kept his arm around me the whole time. I mean like he didn't care who knew. I think I'd have waited forever with his arm around me like that.

Anyway, I'd taken the first pill the night before. It had already started.

Eventually they called us. Inside there was another couple. She was miserable. She cried and cried but I shut her out. I didn't want her there and all that noise was making me crazy. I sat at the table and pretended to read whatever book I had with me. But what I was really doing was hypnotizing myself. I stared at a point and focused on it until I disappeared into myself, until everything inside me slowed down.

I felt humiliated wearing those horrible pads under my sweatpants, sitting with him in that terrible room with that crying girl. So I wished myself away. Stare at the wall and vanish.

If nothing else, we had that in common, I think, our ability to disappear.

He kept touching my hand and asking me if I was O.K., but even *he* started to get on my nerves. I wanted to be absolutely alone or to lose consciousness, to have the thing happen and wake up in his bed. But on the other hand, I was sure that once it was over, he'd leave me.

Then I kept seeing the baby's face. I mean this face I'd imagined for it. Clear. There was a photograph in his apartment of him as a baby with his mother holding him. They were sitting on the beach and his mom, who was so beautiful, was holding him in her arms and he had these big eyes and he was wearing a little white cotton sun hat. And that's what I imagined our baby looked like. Would look like. And no matter how focused I became, no matter how hard I tried to disappear, it was that face that kept bringing me back. I knew it was dead already or dying. I mean I knew that it wasn't a baby, that it wasn't really formed. Still, I kept imagining it struggling inside me. I kept seeing it reaching out for me. And all the time I'm sitting there thinking of its little hands and that pretty round face and *he's* holding my hand saying, Do you need anything, Marie? Are you O.K., Marie? Does it hurt? And I'm thinking, Yes, it hurts. I want to say, Yes, it hurts, Yes. I want to say, I keep seeing the baby and it looks just like you in that photograph in your apartment with your pretty mother and I don't really want to kill it. I want to have it. I want to have it and live with you, the three of us together for the rest of our lives.

But I don't say a thing, I just sit there pretending to be fine, pretending to read.

I don't know how much time passed. Hours I think. And then I started to feel dizzy and feverish. I thought I might vomit. I stood up and as I did a shock of pain went through me hard and my knees nearly gave out. He was looking at me holding my hand sitting there with his face upturned and me standing looking down at him. Everything was spinning. I thought if I moved I'd fall over. I stood looking at him holding his hand until another cramp came. I think I flinched this time because he looked terrified. When I could, I walked to the bathroom. Maybe he came with me. I don't remember. I was very dizzy. There was a lot of blood. I sat doubled over on the toilet with those cramps rippling through me one after another just stabbing away over and over. And then they passed and whatever had been inside me was out. I looked down into the water.

Then I flushed and it was gone.

* * *

It's still hard to believe, but we went to school afterward. We took separate taxis. I spent the day there as if nothing had happened. He taught his classes. Twice I passed him in the halls.

* * *

That afternoon I met him at his apartment. He undressed me and we got into bed and held onto each other. I kept my palm against his chest so I could feel his heart beating. I cried and cried. He stroked my hair and for a long time didn't say anything. He never let go, never shifted. He kept me pressed against his warm body and eventually I was able to take a full breath and slowly I stopped crying. I fell asleep. I was exhausted. I don't know if he slept but when I woke up we hadn't moved. My hand was right there on his chest.

I told him about the baby. I mean the imaginary baby. About how it looked like him. How I thought it looked the way he looked in the photograph with his mother. I said that I loved him. I said, I'm sorry, Will. And he said, You have nothing to be sorry for. We were quiet. Then I told him that I thought I'd miss the baby. I said, That's probably stupid, but I think it's true. He said, It isn't stupid at all.

All of this happened so slowly. The conversation, I mean. One of us would speak and then there'd be a very long pause as we'd both fall asleep for a few minutes and then wake up and say something else. There was a strange quality to the whole evening, like we were drunk or hadn't slept for days, and we lay there for hours just looking up at the beams never at each other.

And then he said, You'll be a wonderful mother someday, Marie. Maybe, I said. But what about you, Will? Don't you want to be a father? He didn't say anything for a long time. I lay there listening to his slow breathing and then he began to cry. I could feel it, and I sat up in bed and looked at him. He was lying there with his eyes closed and he was crying.

Hey, I said as gently as I could. I touched his face. Hey.

But he wouldn't open his eyes. He looked like a kid, like a boy. Will, I said. I kept saying his name.

After a while he opened his eyes and when he did I understood that I didn't know him at all. Because I didn't know what else to say, I said, Will, why are you crying? He said he was sorry that I'd had to go through it. And I told him not to worry about me. That I was sick of talking about me. And he laughed the way someone laughs right in the middle of crying.

He said, Yes. He'd planned on being a father. He said he'd been married for five years. That at the time they were planning on having children.

I looked at him and tried to imagine him married, living with a woman, carrying his child in his arms. And even if I expected it to be hard, I realized that it was easy to imagine. I asked him what had changed and he told me that he'd left his wife and moved to Paris. Or maybe he'd moved to Paris and then left his wife. I don't remember. Why? I asked him. Why would you leave your wife? Weren't you happy?

He lay there and reached out his hand and touched my face and said, I don't know, Marie. And I said, Of course you know, Will. Of course you know. Why would you leave your life like that?

He looked at me for a long time, not speaking, as if he were about to begin a story. I watched him, his mouth slightly open. But he never spoke and slowly he disappeared as fast as he'd come to life.

GILAD

fter school on our first day back from the break, I saw Colin sitting in the small café by the entrance to the *métro*. He was writing with some books and a pack of cigarettes on the table in front of him. I stopped at the top of the stairs and watched him through the glass. He wrote slowly, never taking his eyes away from the page. I was balanced at the edge of the steps between descending into the station and walking into the café. We hadn't spoken much since that Saturday at the protest.

Watching him that afternoon, with people pushing past, I felt again as if I were on the precipice of something. It was as if my life had slowed and accelerated all at once. I thought I'd leave him alone to smoke his cigarettes. But I couldn't stop watching him work, tapping his fingers on the table as he wrote and wrote.

He was a kid writing a paper. He was my friend. The only person who'd never disappointed me. I walked to the café and knocked on the glass. He looked up, raised his chin, and waved me in.

By the time I got through the door and to his table at the window, he'd cleared a space for me. We shook hands—this time traditional, solid, and strong. The waiter came over and I asked for a coffee but Colin said no and ordered us two beers. I shrugged and the waiter left.

"What's this?" I asked glancing at his notebook.

"English."

"Already?"

"I've got things to say, mate. And I want to make sure he fucking reads the thing."

"What do you mean?"

The waiter put our beers in front of us. When he'd gone Colin looked at me. "He won't be around much longer, Gilad."

"Why not?"

"You really *don't* talk to anyone."

"What?"

He picked up his beer and went to take a sip but then stopped. Instead he held his glass up, "Cheers," he said.

"Cheers."

We touched glasses. The low sun was shining through the window onto our table.

"Gilad, man, look, O.K., you know who Marie de Cléry is?"

"I know her. So what?"

"We were together for a long time. I dumped her last year."

"O.K.. So?"

"She's insane and she talks, man. She talks to everyone. She's fucking him. She's fucking Silver, O.K.?"

"Bullshit, Colin," I laughed.

"How do you not know this? You've never heard this story? She hasn't shut up about it."

"You believe it? You're serious?"

"Not at first. At first, I thought it was bullshit but now, mate, I'm pretty sure it's true."

"There's no way it's true."

"I didn't think so either. I mean, fuck, you see the way the girls here follow him around, that guy could have anyone he wants, so why does he choose her? There's no way, right? And I keep shaking my head, thinking there's no way. But now I hear people's parents are talking about it. It's out there, mate."

He took a sip of beer. I looked outside. We sat in silence for a while, watching people funneling from the street into the *métro*. From time to time kids from school would walk past the café and down the stairs, their backpacks slung over their shoulders.

"Look, man, why do you think Ariel hates him so much?"

I shook my head.

"She was the first to find out. She was the first one Marie told, mate. She says she's *morally outraged*. She's so full of shit. All she could talk about last year was how she wanted to get with him. She's just jealous he didn't choose her. We got into a big fucking thing a few months ago. She told me she was going to tell her parents. I told her she was jealous and she lost her shit. When I said that, I didn't even believe it was happening, but now, man, I'm sure it is. Or it was. I even heard she got pregnant."

I watched the street. The sun had fallen behind the trees and the streetlights had come on.

"You think they'll fire him?"

"That's what I hear. I mean, of course they will."

We were quiet for a while. We drank our beers.

"It doesn't matter," Colin said.

I glanced at him, "Why not?"

"I don't know. I've been thinking about the whole thing. Not just the Marie thing, but what he did at the protest. The way he bitched out like that? Let that dickhead spit on him? I don't know. I was mad. I was so fucking mad. Just walked away like that. I expected, I don't know, something more. More . . . more . . ." he trailed off.

"Heroics," I said.

"Heroics," he nodded. "But in the end, at least I learned something from the guy. At least, I don't know. He's not what I thought. Or what I wanted. Maybe he's a disappointment. To you too I know. So he's not a fucking hero. Who is? What do we expect, you know?"

Colin finished his beer. We sat together watching as a woman walked slowly with a cane to the steps of the *métro*. She paused to catch her breath, and then began awkwardly descending the concrete stairs.

"You sound like my mom," I said.

Colin laughed. "Yeah?"

"She asked me the other night, 'What do you expect of people?' As if the only thing we should expect from anyone is disappointment."

"No man, it's just *one* of the things we should expect. But in the end, mate, you're better off not expecting anything. The fucked-up thing is that I still want to write for him. I still want to know what he thinks of what I write, of what I say. Of me, I guess."

"While he's still around," I said.

"While he's still around."

For a while neither of us spoke. Colin stared out at the street and spun his lighter on the table with quick flicks of his wrist. I watched as it turned and turned on the tabletop in a blur of blue.

And then we both watched as Silver came up the street from the school. He walked slowly and alone. His coat was buttoned with the high collar turned up, his gray scarf wound around his throat and his old brown satchel slung over his shoulder. At the steps of the *métro* he stopped. For a moment I thought he might come into the café. Instead he turned and looked back in the direction of the school, then at the Christmas lights still strung across the intersection, and finally higher into the night sky.

Then he turned and vanished into the *métro*.

* * *

Soon I was on the boulevard St. Germain walking home. The cafés were crowded. The sharp night air smelled like chestnuts and burning sugar. It seemed a long time since I'd noticed any of it. The entire boulevard was lined with blue lights.

From the hall I heard voices in the apartment. I slid my key into the lock and opened the door. My mother sat facing the fire, her arms spread out behind her, a glass of champagne in her left hand. She was wearing jeans and a heavy white turtleneck sweater, her legs folded beneath her. She was laughing when I walked into the room, her mouth slightly open, her eyes fixed on my father in a black suit and a light-pink shirt. There was no tie. He held a bottle of champagne in one hand and a glass in the other. He was smiling.

"Come on, Gilad, it's cold out there," he said.

I closed the door behind me. The warmth of the room, the low lights, my parents there, the fire, it felt so familiar. I wanted to collapse into the couch next to my mother, take off my shoes, lean against her, give in.

"Do you want to sit down, sweetheart?" she asked, touching her fingers to the place next to her.

I stood, pretending I wasn't grateful for the warmth, for the fire, for the music.

"You want a glass of champagne, kiddo?" He lifted the bottle into the air.

I looked at him. His eyebrows raised, a slight smirk on his square face, his dull eyes. "Have a glass," he said. "Welcome me home."

"Gilad," she said, "take your coat off, come sit next to me."

I turned to her, took off my coat and dropped it with my bag on the floor. I sat next to her. She wrapped her arm around me and squeezed my shoulder. I stared into the fire trying not to blink.

"No," I said. "No champagne."

"Go on, honey," she said. "It'll do you some good."

"A peace offering," he said, raising the bottle again.

I turned from the fire toward him. "A peace offering?"

He walked to the fireplace and rested the bottle on the mantelpiece. "I know you're angry with me, Gilad. We'll have a glass of champagne and let it go, O.K.?"

"It?" I asked, looking up at him.

He sighed and shook his head. The smirk was gone along with his momentary joviality. "The whole fucking thing, Gilad. We'll just let it go. Why do you always have to be so sour? We were having a lovely time here before you showed up with your little mood."

"What's the thing you'd like to forget, exactly?" I was sweating and my mom must have felt it through my shirt. My heart was beating hard.

"Gilad," she whispered.

From the fireplace he reached for the standing lamp just to my left and flicked the switch so the room filled with a harsh light.

"The thing I want to forget, Gilad, is how whiny you are." He looked down at me. I looked back at him.

"Michael," my mother said.

"What?" he asked, looking at her angrily.

"Turn off the light, please."

"I want to look at our son," he said. "Come on Gilad, kiss and make up? Make your mother happy?"

He kept his fingers on the switch. There beneath that white light, I studied his hand. In spite of his manicured fingers, his skin had begun to wrinkle and break in hundreds of lines around his knuckles.

I smiled.

"Good," he said. "Finally."

I laughed.

"What's so funny?"

I stood up.

We were close there, tucked in between the couch and the fading fire, his back nearly touching the mantle. I looked him full in the face. He was an old man. His eyes were tired. His skin had begun to fall from his jaw. There were deepening lines across his forehead. When was the last time I'd been this close to him? When had his hair gone so gray?

"You look old," I said quietly.

"What?"

"You've gotten old." I looked straight at him.

He shook his head as if I were crazy.

"It isn't complicated. You look old. You're an old man."

He straightened. "Watch your mouth."

"I hadn't noticed before, but with the light, it's incredible. You're an old man now." My voice was steady.

Like that. It was gone. I could see my father, standing there, dying. As if I were watching the end of a life. I imagined him aging to death in front of me. His skin wrinkling, his spine curving forward, his rotten teeth falling from his mouth.

"Another word you little fuck," he whispered.

"And what? You're going to hit your wife again?"

He moved toward me but I pressed my hands against his chest, pushed him back hard against the mantelpiece and held him there. Neither of us moved. I could feel his heart beating through his clean, pressed shirt, his skin warm. We looked at each other until I pulled my hands away.

I reached beneath the lampshade, turned off the light, touched her shoulder and went to my room.

That night in bed I could still feel his chest warm against my hands.

289

MARIE

F or weeks he took care of me. Every possible moment I could spend with him, I did. He cooked for me. He put me in the bath and washed my back. He brought me flowers. You've never seen a more attentive man. But he barely spoke and the feeling that he was fading away, that he might not even fully exist, was stronger than ever.

Then he was gone.

It was Ariel who told me.

I was sitting alone at a table in the library at the end of the day.

She came in and said, I'm so sorry, Marie. I looked at her and didn't know what she meant. She crouched down next to me, put her hand on my knee and said, her face full of false compassion: Mr. Silver. They fired him. I just stared at her. I didn't say a thing. She touched my hand. Are you O.K., Marie? I didn't tell anyone, she said. I swear to God, Marie.

I stood up and left.

Mr. Spencer stopped me in the hall.

He said we needed to talk. He took me to his office and asked me if it was true. And I said I didn't know what he was talking about. He said, You don't have to lie. You don't have to protect him. And then the head of the school came in. I'd never talked to her before. I can't remember her name. She sat next to me and put her arm around my shoulder and said, You're the victim here, Marie, and we're going to do every-thing we can to take care of you. She said, You're never going to have to worry about him again. He'll never touch you again. He'll never be back here. Never.

I pulled my chair away so that she couldn't touch me. Mr. Spencer said they needed to talk to my parents. He picked up the phone and called my mother and asked her to come to school. There was a pause and then he said, It's about your daughter.

Then he said, Well, I'd prefer to have the conversation in person. He waited. O.K., well there's only one way to say this, Madame de Cléry, your daughter has had a sexual relationship with a teacher. One of our teachers. He nodded and hung up the phone.

I guess she can't get to school today, he said. He gave the head of the school a look. Then he said to me, We'd like you to see the psychologist before going home. I didn't know what he meant by we, if it was we the school or we the school and my mother.

I told him that I needed to leave. That I needed to go home. That I had a paper to write. The head of the school said she didn't want me to be alone as if I'd kill myself or something. I got up to go, but when I turned around there was Ms. Carver standing in the doorway. She gave me one of those bullshit looks and hugged me and said, I'm so sorry. Oh sweetie I'm so sorry.

I said, What for? She said, For what he did to you. I said, What do you mean? And she said, Sweetie, you don't have to pretend anymore. You don't have to protect him. It's all over now. It's all over. You're safe.

I tried to leave but they wouldn't let me go. The head of the school said that legally they couldn't leave me alone. That after something like this they'd need me to be picked up by a loved one.

A loved one.

Where is he? I asked. Where's Will?

The head of the school told me that he'd left the campus that afternoon. That he'd been fired. I wanted to cry. Instead, I concentrated on hating them.

I took my phone out of my bag and listened to my messages. They didn't stop me. He'd called. He was very calm and spoke so softly it was hard to hear. Everyone in the room watched me, listening, waiting for me to say something. I listened twice and then I erased it. Goodbye Marie, he said. I'm sure you've heard. I don't think we'll see each other for a while.

Mr. Spencer took me home. He kept saying that I'd be O.K. That everything would work out for the best. When we got there he insisted on walking me to the door. He wanted to talk to my mother but she wasn't home. I didn't ask him in and eventually he left.

My mother never talked about it, either. She never said a word to me. I don't think she even told my father. If she had, he'd have called at least. Maybe he wouldn't have said anything about it, but at least he would have called.

Then everything you'd imagine happened. At school I mean. There was the predictable chaos. They all stared at me. Ariel tried to talk to me. I ignored her. I tried not to pay attention. By then, I felt so numb. It was like this wild rush of noise and excitement was swirling all around me and I was motionless. I felt drugged. I called him and called him. I wrote. But he never responded. I went to his apartment and rang but he didn't answer. I sat in the café across the street and waited for hours. The lights never came on. He never went in. He never came out. I went back a lot. But there was never a sign of life.

* * *

I suppose in the end the way he left was as good as any other. I like to think he did it for me, that he thought it was the best way.

I don't know.

They made me see Ms. Carver once a week until the end of the year. What a fraud. I couldn't stand her. She said he used me. That he needed to assert his power. She kept saying it, He needed to assert his power. He took advantage of you, Marie. Do you understand that? He took advantage of you. Do you understand? You must understand that. You have to understand it for you to heal. God she loved that word—heal.

And I'd say, No, Ms. Carver I don't understand that. And she'd say, But you must be angry at him. He abandoned you. Don't you see that he used you? You must be angry. You *should* be angry. I'd turn away from her and look out the window. Even if I'd been angry, and I guess I was, I wouldn't have given her the pleasure, you know? She was so smug, so pleased with herself, sitting in her big chair looking at me from under all that makeup like she had the whole thing figured out, as if without her help I wouldn't survive.

Sometimes I'd talk to Ms. Keller. In the beginning I went to her because I thought maybe she knew where he was, maybe she'd take me to him. But she didn't know. At first I thought she was lying. But you could see how sad she was. I started to think she was the only other person in the world who could understand. I could see how much it hurt her. She listened. She never tried to convince me he was a bad person. Still, I'm sure she felt betrayed by him and angry and embarrassed.

People thought she knew all along. Ms. Carver practically said so. But he never told anyone. And all you had to do was look at Ms. Keller's face and you'd know. She was wrecked. I think maybe she'd been in love with him. Once when we were alone in her classroom she cried.

I kept asking her, Where is he? You must know, I said. But she just looked at me and shook her head and when I saw how upset she was, I stopped asking. That's when she started to cry. She wiped her eyes and said, I'm sorry, Marie.

She was always there when I needed her. I didn't even think about it then, but now I realize she was probably angry at me too.

We'd betrayed her, and even if she was a teacher and I was a student it didn't really matter. I'd lied to her and it's like I said before, we all came to the same place every day. We were part of one another's lives. They were like us and we were like them.

* * *

I don't know what happened to him. Where he went or ended up. I imagine that he went home, back to his wife, where they picked up their lives and had a child together. Sometimes I think about them sitting on an empty beach somewhere. Maybe a beach in Brittany in late autumn. The three of them all alone. I can see them there in the sun.

I still dream about him.

WILL

One morning there is a note on my desk. "Will, Please meet me in Laetitia's office. Paul."

* * *

I walk over to the gym where a game is underway. I can hear the familiar hollow pounding of basketballs against the smooth gym floor.

The kids with free periods are packed into the wooden bleachers. Julia waves at me from her seat in the back row. I smile at her and she makes a show of finding me a place to sit, sliding over against Lydia. I make my way through the crowd. There are parents scattered around, cheering their kids on as they charge up and down the court.

"What's up, Silver?" Lydia asks never looking away from the game.

"Oh my God, Mr. Silver, the game's so close." Julia elbows me in the side, watching as an American School of London player makes a free throw.

I watch Rick, his eyes on the basket, waiting for the rebound. I see him in class, fiercely scrutinizing the board. The shot misses. Julia screams in delight. I look out across the court and scan the opposite bleachers.

The game is close and with each basket the gym becomes louder.

There are two minutes left to play.

The fans stomp their feet and the small gym shakes. I watch a middle-school student cup his hands around his mouth and scream for his school. Girls on the London side holding a banner: "London Rocks!"

The bright fluorescent lights hang high above. The crowd seems to undulate and move in unison. A single body. And not only the crowd but also the players flowing from end to end, the ball flying through the air, from hand to hand.

Let's go London, let's go. Stomp stomp. Let's go London, let's go. Stomp stomp.

I. S. F., we chant. I. S. F.

I am pressed in with the rest of them, cheering every Paris basket and beneath those bright humming lights I'm absorbed by the joyous crowd.

Then with a minute left in the game we call a time out.

The clock is frozen at 58 seconds.

The players huddle around their respective coaches. Julia punches my shoulder.

"Oh my God, Mr. Silver," she says hitting me again.

Lydia rolls her eyes.

I look up to find Paul Spencer watching me from across the court.

I look back and meet his eyes.

ISF wins the game at the buzzer.

Around me the crowd rises. Everyone is standing. He can no longer see me.

For a moment I stay there beneath them, surrounded, their noise far away.

Then I get up and touch Julia's shoulder.

"I'll see you later," I whisper.

"We won, Mr. Silver! We won!"

"It's great," I say. "Bye, Lydia. I'll see you."

She smiles at me. "See you, Silver."

I climb down through the crowd, out of the bleachers and onto the gym floor. I slip through the doors, and toward the entrance where Mazin is standing with Steven Connor.

"Hey Mr. Silver," Steven says.

"Hi, Steve. How are you, Maz?"

He shrugs and turns away.

I look at him until he faces me.

"Say what you have to say, Mazin."

"Nothing to say."

I wait a moment.

"O.K. I'll see you guys."

I squeeze Mazin's shoulder and walk outside away from the fading roar.

I stop at the picnic table beneath the pine tree and sit with my feet on the bench. I feel very still.

I regret that I haven't said some kind of good-bye.

I think of all those kids I've taught spread throughout the building.

I want to find Mazin again. I want to explain to him. To all of them. To Mike Chandler, to Jane and Lydia and Hala and Julia and Colin and Gilad.

But what's the difference really? Whatever I've done for them, whatever I haven't, all of it is finished. In the end, leaving them with an image of a small white dog limping across a field of snow isn't so much worse than a grand good-bye.

I call Marie. She doesn't answer. I leave a message.

"Marie, it's me," I say. "I don't know what's next for you exactly but the weeks ahead will be horrible. I'm sorry for that. You're so much braver than I am. Anyway, Marie, it was coming. You knew that. So, here it is. And maybe, I don't know, it'll be a relief. Maybe, maybe. Please take care of yourself. We'll see each other one day. But not for a while, I don't think."

I return to the English department where I collect my things—a file of personal letters from students and parents. A few books. My coffee mug.

After all that time, there isn't much I can see keeping.

I lean against my desk and listen to voices fade in the halls as the school empties.

I leave most of it the way it is.

Red pens in the drawer alongside a box of staples, grade book on my desk for whoever will replace me.

Mia's coat and scarf are draped across the back of her chair. Everyone else has left with the last bell, or is in the gym celebrating, but she's working with the kids to prepare the winter issue of the literary magazine. She'll be there late, hidden away in the computer lab, making final decisions about the latest round of submissions.

I imagine her in that low-lit room, monitors glowing, illuminating our small, faithful club.

She is at her best among those kids who love her. There she is the center of the world, arbiter of taste, patient reader, sharp critic, legislator of perfect moral order.

I sit at her desk and take one of her red ballpoint pens from the drawer and begin to write.

Dear Mia,

But I can't muster it and leave it there, just those two words across a sheet of white paper: "Dear Mia,"

I get up. I touch her coat hanging from the back of the chair and leave the office.

* * *

From the hallway I can see Moore sitting in a chair facing an empty gray couch. On either end are two matching chairs.

There's Mr. Al Mady in one, left leg crossed over his bent right knee so that I can see the worn sole of his shoe. I walk through the door and my entrance freezes a smile on his face.

Paul Spencer is in the chair facing him.

Moore turns to me as if she too is surprised to find me there. I think I've made a mistake. Perhaps they've changed their minds. For a moment I feel relieved but before I can speak, before I relax, before I give in to it, she says stiffly, "Come in, Will."

I take the place that's been prepared for me on the low couch. I wonder if this suite of furniture is new. I don't remember it.

Paul Spencer sits rubbing his hand against his beard. Moore faces me, dressed in a beige suit. She's rigid, sitting with her legs crossed. Behind her I can see the parking lot through the window. The last buses are pulling away. Omar Al Mady, to my right, has shifted in his chair so that his body is turned slightly in my direction.

I'm breathing shallow breaths and sitting forward on the edge of the couch. I can feel the blood pulsing slowly through the veins in my neck. I'm entirely present. It's a strange sensation, bordering, I think for a moment, on joy.

"Will," she says. "I'd like to ask you a question."

I nod.

"I'm just going to be direct here. I imagine you know what this is about and that the question won't come as a surprise to you."

She looks from side to side, first at Al Mady and then at Paul Spencer. And then back at me.

"Will," she says. "Are you now having or have you ever had an inappropriate relationship with a student enrolled at this school?"

I stay still. I don't say anything. I only lower my eyes from her mouth to the glass table in front of me. I wait.

I feel my heart beating. I imagine the blood moving through my body. In all the time I've had to think about it, I've never considered my answer.

I focus my eyes on the reflection of the overhead light in the glass. It seems to brighten and take on depth and texture.

I don't know how much time I let pass.

"Will," Paul Spencer says.

"No," I say and quickly raise my eyes to his. I think he's disappointed in me, that he'd been hoping, at least, if nothing else, that I'd be honest.

Mr. Al Mady uncrosses his legs and sits forward as if he's about to speak.

Moore says, "We have evidence. Other students who have come forward."

Her voice is unsteady. She speaks quietly, but beneath the slow control there is rage. I know she hates me, that she sees me as an evil man who's violated a young woman. I'm a hypocrite and a liar. I'm a child abuser.

"Will," Paul Spencer says again, this time softly, the way a good father might urge his son to stop crying, to get back into the game, to stop lying and tell the truth.

"Yes," I say, and raise my eyes. "Yes," I say again.

"Ah," Al Mady says nodding his head and placing both his feet on the floor. "Yes."

"O.K.," she says. "You are released from your position here. The best thing for you and for Marie and for us, Will, is to leave at the end of the school day, the way you normally would. And then tomorrow you won't come back."

"Will," Spencer says.

I look at him.

"It's a terrible thing you've done. You must know that. The school, it will take a long time for the school to recover. A lot of people cared about you here. But then you know all this."

He shakes his head.

I'm silent.

After a moment Moore opens a white folder.

"Well," she says withdrawing a sheet of paper. She places it on the table.

I stare at it laid out on the glass.

"This cuts you from the school. Officially. Sign and it's over and beginning tomorrow, you will no longer be employed here," Al Mady says leaning forward, straining to read as if to be sure it's the correct document. He removes a gold Cartier pen from his jacket pocket and places it on the table. "After you sign you're free, Mr. Silver."

I take the strap of my bag and wind it around my fist so that I have something to hold on to.

"You must realize that what you've done is wrong, Will. Don't you want to say anything?" Moore asks, shaking her head.

I look at her and feel that I'm drowning.

I want to say something about Marie—her cool skin smelling like night, the way she looked those dim winter mornings, how brave she is, but I realize it will only make them angrier.

I open my bag and withdraw a plastic ballpoint pen.

I brush the gold pen to the side. It clatters as it rolls across the glass.

I sign the paper.

She returns it to the folder.

They all seem relieved.

Al Mady retrieves his pen. I leave mine on the table.

He says, "Mr. Silver, a question if you'll permit me?"

I meet his eyes for the first time since arriving in the room.

"I wonder—perhaps I don't understand—but is it true that you're not sorry for what you've done? Morally. Are you sorry? I mean, fundamentally. Do you regret what you've done here? Or are you utterly unrepentant? Do you understand that what you've done is wrong?"

I've wrapped the strap tighter around my hand. I hold his

eyes for a moment, and then turn toward Paul Spencer. I am surprised to find him looking at me hopefully, as if he too wants an answer to the same question.

All of them are watching me so intently.

I get up and am struck by how different I feel standing there looking down at them.

I think I see a flash of fear in Moore's eyes and it occurs to me that she's worried I might become violent.

They look at me from all sides until I leave them there.

* * *

I walk down the hall, through the foyer and through the gates, where there is nearly no daylight left. The moon is a bright crescent in the cold evening sky and somehow I feel ready to live my life again. I stop at the end of that familiar street. I look back in the direction of the school and then up at the Christmas lights strung across the intersection. Then I look higher, beyond those pale electric lights, to the darkening sky.

ACKNOWLEDGMENTS

To Pascale Brevet, whose love, grace, elegance, and courage have kept me alive for years and years.

To Merritt Tierce and Dorothy Royle, relentless friends and readers whose generosity and talent astound me.

To Jon Brockett, Erik Leidecker, Gretchen Wagner, James Tooley, John McNulty, Grant Rosenberg, Lianne Halfon, Jane Lewty, Andy Scisco, John Heintz, Ellen Adams, Martina Bacigalupo, Adriano Valerio, Sahngmie Lah, Anthony Marra and Ayana Mathis for their tireless support and kindness.

To Eric Simonoff, for his patience, wisdom, and generosity, and for refusing to give up on me.

To Alice Sebold, for her passion and unwavering faith. Reader and editor of my dreams.

To John Burnham Schwartz—mentor and friend.

To Bob Brock, Paul Hoornbeek, Ethan Canin, and Allan Gurganus—the four teachers who mattered.

309

To Tom Jenks, who was there first.

Thank you also to Susanna Moore, Naomi Shihab Nye, Bibliothèque Mazarine, Alixe Turner, Ziad Musallam, Claire Peverelli, the Biles family, Sophie Maarleveld, Elisabeth Hofmann, Doyeun Kim, Fernando Laposse, Michael Reynolds, Heather Bensko, Brad Listi, Steven Younger, Elena Calabrese, Luca Younger, Bob Goodkind, David Barnes, Cabaret Populaire, and the Iowa Writers' Workshop.